CONFESSIONS OF A JACKBOY 2

Lock Down Publications & Ca$h
Presents
Confessions of a Jackboy 2
A Novel by *Nicholas Lock*

Lock Down Publications
P.O. Box 944
Stockbridge, Ga 30281

Visit our website at www.lockdownpublica-
tions.com

Book interior design by: **Shawn Walker**
Edited by: **Nuel Uyi**

Nicholas Lock

Stay Connected with Us!

Text **LOCKDOWN** to 22828 to stay up-to-date with new releases, sneak peaks, contests and more…

Thank You

Submission Guideline

Submit the first three chapters of your completed manuscript to ldpsubmissions@gmail.com, subject line: Your book's title. The manuscript must be in a .doc file and sent as an attachment. Document should be in Times New Roman, double spaced and in size 12 font. Also, provide your synopsis and full contact information. If sending multiple submissions, they must each be in a separate email.

Have a story but no way to send it electronically? You can still submit to LDP/Ca$h Presents. Send in the first three chapters, written or typed, of your completed manuscript to:

LDP: Submissions Dept
Po Box 944
Stockbridge, Ga 30281

*DO NOT send original manuscript. Must be a duplicate. *

Provide your synopsis and a cover letter containing your full contact information.

Thanks for considering LDP and Ca$h Presents.

Nicholas Lock

Chapter One

Kameesha surviving the torture I had put her through and three shots at point-blank range was either a miracle or someone was praying for her because I had definitely tried to send her to the afterlife. The same could be said for me as well because I had been catching break after break since I survived the five shots Kameesha's brother—Ghost—had hit me with. Now it looked as if I was going to beat the two murder charges and the attempted murder charges. With Cynthia's dad presiding over my case, I knew I didn't have a worry in the world. His wink assured me of that. He had told me that he was holding me responsible for Cynthia's safety. And I hadn't upheld my end of the bargain by allowing Rude Boy to kill her and our unborn daughter. But when I walked out of jail, I was going straight to Golden Creek to shoot somebody's son. The only reason Rude Boy was still breathing was because I was locked up. It was gonna be a bloodbath. I had plans on making it rain blood! Rude Boy probably thought his act of killing Cynthia and our daughter was going to go unpunished with me locked in a cell and my niggas not gunning for him. But them not gunning for him was by design. Rude Boy was to die by my hands only. He had taken my voice of reason when he killed Cynthia. I was content before with flying below the radar, but now Face was about to become a household name.

While they got everything in order, I turned towards Rai'chell and asked: "Why you playing games?"

"I don't know what you're talking about." She played dumb.

"He looks just like me," I nodded at the baby in her lap.

"Boy, you know that's your son," Diqueena butted in, and I looked at Rai'chell.

"Mr. Lowe, your case has been continued," the bailiff informed me.

"Bring my son to see me. Today!" I stood up.

Before I walked out of the courtroom, I looked at Judge Weeks, but he was looking over some legal papers. So I kept it pushing.

During the entire ride back to the county jail, I was lost in my thoughts. Why had Rai'chell lied about whose baby she was carrying? She had gone a little too far with that one. I got back to the county and rushed to my block. I needed to be there when Rai'chell came. I wasn't trying to miss her visit. We had a lot to discuss.

"What happened, buddy?" Ox asked me as I came through the sally port. He had gotten back before me.

"The exact thing that I told you was going to happen, a continuance." I walked to my cell.

"I got something to take your mind off that courtroom." Ox headed towards his cell.

Since coming to the county, I had took a liking to Ox. We clicked instantly. That was rare among young niggas, especially two alphas. Then we were in HBB—one of the *high band blacks*—which was also the block where they kept the dudes that were under eighteen. The bottom floor was mainly for the niggas that weren't yet eighteen, and the top floor was the murder floor. You had to have a murder charge to be housed there. Put the killers and the young boys together, and you can imagine the hostile environment it created. It was really a concrete jungle that housed lions, tigers, bears, snakes, and rats. And a bunch of hyenas; these were the dudes that had to have their homeboys with them to go hard. Me and Ox were cut from the same cloth. We were both wolves. He was just like me. Young, reckless and living for the moment. Ox was only sixteen but he had the hard, cold eyes of someone twice his age. Someone who had weathered the many storms that life threw at him and had come out on top. At his young age, Ox was already a vet in the streets. With his mom being a junky and his dad missing, Ox was forced to fend for himself. At 5'8 and a hundred and sixty pounds, Ox didn't cast an imposing figure, but his name wasn't Ox for no reason. He was strong as an Ox and mean as a rattlesnake. Then Ox had a crew of young boys that was just like him. They called themselves the Turban Gang. Word made the rounds that they were a branch of the Taliban—those that sported full beards as did Ox, and it was mandatory that you have a turban. Their sole mission was simply to terrorize shit! It didn't matter who you were. That's what Ox had been doing when the police had ran down on him. Ox was robbing a couple at an ATM when the police pulled up on him. The minute the police opened their doors, Ox started letting his hammer talk. Ox didn't have no picks. He would let anybody have it, but the couple he'd been robbing picked him out of a line-up, earning him a vacation to the county jail and facing the death penalty.

"You got some brown paper?" Ox asked, walking into my room.

"Yea, what you got?"

Brown paper was what we used to roll up in. It was nothing more than a brown paper towel soaked in coffee, which created a slow burning blunt wrap.

"You already know." Ox tossed a bag of weed in my lap. I rolled up a healthy blunt of gas, and took a few pulls. I sat back and let the weed invade my system.

"Y'all need to light an incense in there." Ms. Gipson poked her head in my room

Ms. Gipson was a C.O. and was cool as hell. She could care less what we did, as long as we didn't hurt anybody.

"I got you, Ms. G," I said.

"She on you, bro," Ox said when she walked off. "She never even looked my way."

"I ain't sweating that bitch, bro."

Ms. Gipson was about thirty-seven, 5'9, 160 pounds, dark brown-skinned with round, shapely breasts and an ass that poked out just right on her slim frame.

"I'm gon' tell you something I learned. Opportunities don't come around often for a nigga, especially one that's locked up. So when you see one, it's in our best interest to grab it. You never know what can come from it."

There was some truth to his words.

"Lowe, you have a visit," Ms. Gipson's voice came through on the intercom in my room.

"I'll be back," I said to Ox. He nodded.

The weed coursing through my body put my initial plan of snapping on Rai'chell on hold. The loud had me mellow, but I was still going to get on her about lying to me. I sat down in the visitation area, waiting for the screen to pop on. Our visits were done on a computer screen. When Rai'chell's cinnamon-brown face popped up on the screen, all her past transgressions were forgiven. I don't know what it was, but she had that kind of effect on me. Ever since I had met her five years ago, she had a hold on my heart. It was like she'd tattooed her name on it.

"Where my son at?"

"He's in the car with Diqueena. He was getting sleepy, so he was being fussy. I didn't want to bring him in here crying. Besides, we need to talk."

"You're right. Why the fuck did you feel the need to lie about being pregnant by Jaden?"

I got mad all over again.

"I did that to make you mad. You completely left me alone when we broke up. It was like you stopped loving me the instant we broke up." Rai'chell's eyes began to get misty.

"Chell, I never stopped loving you. I don't think that's possible for me," I admitted grudgingly.

"Your mama been knew that Nymel Junior was her grandchild," she grinned slyly. "She was there when I had him. She told me she was going to let me tell you on my own." I was stunned by Rai'chell's confession. I was going to holler at my mom about this bit of information.

"And just so your big head ass know, because I know how your ass think, me and Jaden didn't really fuck. I made him stop after a few minutes. I didn't feel right allowing someone else to be inside of me."

"You named him Nymel, huh? How do he be acting? Is he anything like me?" I switched the topic.

"He only four months! All he really do is sleep. We can discuss Nymel later. What's up with us? We have a child together. Are we going to make this thing work or nah?" She looked at me with her arched brow raised.

"What do you wanna do?"

"If you're giving me a choice, we're going to be in a serious relationship. I'm the wifey and will be treated as such."

"Chell, I don't have a problem making you my wifey, but baby, considering the life I'm living right now, wifeing you up right now would only make you and my son a target."

"Nigga, I'm built for this shit! I'm not that same little girl you met in middle school. I'm grown now. When you were getting baptized into the streets, I was too. Only I was doin' it through you and your experiences. You jumped off the porch, and I walked off right behind you. I was there for you through thick and thin. I can't go into detail because they're recording this but know I was there for Jim." She reminded me of some

11

shit no one knew. "So know there's no way for a woman to deal with a man on an intimate level for years at a time and not soak up the game unless she a bird ass bitch. I'm not saying I'm all the way like that, but I can handle myself. Nigga, that's why they made sidewalks because everybody ain't built for the streets!" Rai'chell glared at me defiantly

My boo had gotten some heart, and I liked it.

"I hear that gangsta shit you talking, but I need you to know that it's a lot easier when you're on the sidelines watching the game. But when you get the nerve to step inside that motherfucka, you see it's the dirtiest, grimiest, most treacherous place on earth. It will chew your pretty ass up and spit you out. It's really *trust no man or bitch* for that matter. But you don't have to worry about that. All I need you to do is, sit on my lap and look pretty."

Beep! *Beep*! *Beep*! The monitor flashed three times, letting us know we only had sixty seconds left.

"You need to call Murph too. Rude Boy shot his car up and he wrecked it," she said, and the screen went black.

I immediately went and got on one of the four phones in the block to call Murph. He pressed *five* asap. I wasn't able to get a word out before Murph went in.

"Bra, that nigga gotta get his issue! He caused me to flip that motherfucka! I understand you want him yourself but they went on offense after you got locked up and haven't slowed down." Murph's voiced was laced with undiluted anger.

"Handle your business then."

"And kick your feet up and relax. You should be out in the next two months. I got you a lawyer and Angie said if you don't call her today, it's smoke."

"I'm about to hit her right now." I hung up and called Angie.

She replicated Murph and went in before I could talk.

"Face, your black ass ain't called me in two days!"

"Aw, you miss daddy's voice? For real though, Angie, I be so caught up trying to orchestrate shit I just be forgetting," I said apologetically.

"Don't stress, baby. I got a plan to get you out of there. You gon' be proud of me," she said with conviction.

I was getting ready to respond when the sally port opened, and Rude Boy's bitch ass walked in.

Nicholas Lock

Chapter Two

I hung the phone up on Angie and went to my room. I didn't want Rude Boy to see me just yet. The only thing Rude Boy deserved was a slow death. Killing him in jail would almost guarantee me a life sentence, so I was just going to blow him. That way, every day he looked in the mirror and see the scars on his face, he would be reminded of me.

"Why you run to your room like that?" Ox stood in my doorway.

"That's Rude that just came in. I had to come get my knife. I'm about to give that nigga the business."

"Nah, fam, I got you. You got enough going on. Besides, I got some new terrorists that haven't earned their stripes yet. What better way to have them pledge their loyalty to the squad than to draw some blood! Face, when I say I fuck with a nigga, that's what it is. One hand washes the other. You have a legit chance at being a free man again. I don't. The evidence against me is too strong. I have a team of terrorists in the streets at my disposal, and you need them. All I want you to do is, keep it real with a nigga. I read this quote by Ulysses S. Grant that said, *The friend in my adversity I shall always cherish most. I can better trust those who helped to relieve the gloom of my dark hours than those who are so ready to enjoy with me the sunshine of my prosperity.*" Ox showed me another side of him.

Being incarcerated tended to do that to certain niggas. It caused niggas to think more and read more. Something we didn't do enough of while we were in the streets. I do know that the last thing the streets wanted was for me to come home and add some retarded young boys to the team. The city wasn't ready for that.

"I appreciate it, Ox, but I put in my work. That way, I know it will get done the right way and I ain't got to worry about a nigga telling on me."

"Oh bitch, you tried my gang! Sit back and watch the turban show. Yo—Vicious, Trauma, come here real quick." Ox called two of his homies to my room. "That nigga that just came in need his dome checked. Take the door plates."

Door plates were knives made out of the metal plate on the inside of the door

"And that snitching gene doesn't exist in my gang's blood. They all know beforehand that to rat means to not only forfeit your life but your families as well. Of course we've had one that didn't take his vows serious."

"There's always going to be people who find it easier to speak vows than to uphold them," I said.

Ox shrugged. "We had one of our young terrorists decide it was in his best interest to join the *help yourself program* and tell about a gas station robbery. You may have seen it in the paper or on the news. Family gruesomely murdered in their home community reeling. Killer still at large. Since then we haven't had any issues."

Me and Ox watched as Vicious and Trauma left my room to go grab their knives. Rude Boy was putting the mattress cover on his mat when the young boys entered his room. He put up a fight, but it was futile. The knives were too big and they were coming too fast and too frequently.

"Tali! Tali! Tali!" Ox yelled their war cry, sending the two into a frenzy.

Somehow, Rude Boy managed to fight his way out of the room.

His orange jumpsuit was tattered and bloody.

"10-40! 10-40! HBB! 10-40! HBB!" Ms. Gipson yelled the code for a fight into her radio.

Rude Boy wobbled and fell unconscious on the ground. Vicious and Trauma started nailing him to the floor. I tell you, they were doing him bad! Every time one of them would bring their knife down, you could hear it hitting the floor. So, every swing was sending the knife all the way through Rude Boy's body. One thing I could say though was that he didn't holler. He took the brutal stabbing like a champ.

Watching Rude Boy lay helpless as the blood drained out his body was therapeutic though, but I still wouldn't be content until he no longer had breath in his body.

"Turban gang! Tali! Tali! Put your motherfuckin' turbans in the air!" Ox yelled, and half the bottom floor began to cut up.

I didn't know it was that many of them in the block.

"Face, all my people give it up just like that, no questions asked, just go mode. Tell me you couldn't use us on your team." Ox spoke into the vent from his room; they'd made us lock down

"We gon' see, my nigga, we gon' see."

I fell asleep with visions of Rude Boy laying in a pool of his own blood.

"Lowe! Lowe! Face!" Ms. Gipson yelled into the intercom, waking me up.

"Yea." I sat up.

"You have a visit."

I got up, washed my face and brushed my teeth.

"Boy, you ain't got to get all pretty. It ain't like it's a woman coming to see you." Ms. Gipson stuck her head in my room.

"And she gon' be blood raw," I bragged. "You must don't know who you're talking to."

She looked me up and down and rolled her eyes before strutting off. I walked to the visitation area and grabbed one of the empty seats. I was getting lucky because we were only supposed to get one visit a day. I picked the phone up, and Pocahontas's pretty face popped up.

"Hey, Face! You doing okay in there?" she asked, concerned.

"What's up? What are you doing here?"

"I came to talk to you."

I balled my face up.

"Not like that, boy! I came to talk to you about the strip club."

"You can't let it go to waste. Cynthia would go crazy."

"That's where I come in. I can run it until you get out and if you're satisfied with my services, you can keep me. I'm still gonna be dancing too." Pocahontas sounded confident.

This was definitely a good idea. I could get paid while I sat on my ass. And Cynthia would go loony if nothing came of *Pleasure's Paradise*. She had put a lot into the club to get me to invest into it. So, I would be disrespecting her memory by not continuing with the strip club.

"I like that idea but know this—Pocahontas, I don't play about my money," I said sincerely. "Keep everything on the up and up, and we'll be good."

"Always. I'm gonna get on that as soon as I leave. Do you need anything?"

"Hell yea! Freedom, a phone, some Henny. It's a bunch that I need but nothing you can help me with." I leaned over to check out the girl on the screen beside me.

"You underestimate me but I got you," Pocahontas said, brimming with confidence.

"We gonna find out."

I hung up the phone and stood up. I walked up to the desk to holler at Ms. Gipson when she put the phone she had to her ear down and said: "Mr. Lowe, you have an attorney visit. Come on so I can put these shackles on you."

I let her put them on, then walked out the sally port out of the block. There was a pretty redbone waiting on me in the room they did attorney visits.

"No way you're my lawyer."

"Yes, your homeboy Murph hired me yesterday. I'm Tasha Whitlock. There's a little bit I need to know about you so I can get started on your case." She looked down at the stock of papers in front of her, nibbling on the pen in her hand.

I was checking her physique out while she was talking, and I was impressed. She was well put together. She stood about 6'0, weighed about 200 pounds, with light brown eyes, and shapely boobs, and I could tell she had a super fat ass even with her sitting down.

"Mr. Lowe, my eyes are way up here." She scrunched her face up.

I was about to give her a reality check because it was obvious she wasn't used to dealing with niggas of my caliber. She probably assumed since I was only eighteen, I was acting like the typical eighteen-year-old.

"Yo shawty, let's get one thing straight right now. You need me, I don't need you. I'm gonna beat this case with or without you."

"What do you mean?" she said.

"No witnesses, no case," I replied. I hoped she got the underlying meaning.

"So when you get your shit together, come see me. Until then, I don't wanna see you." I walked out, not giving her a chance to respond.

"Don't come back in here with that frown on your face," Ms. Gipson joked, but she had caught me at the wrong time.

"Bitch, if you're not trying to do nothing to turn this frown upside down, then mind your business." I walked off on her too.

I was taking off my jumpsuit when my door opened, and Ms. Gipson stepped in the doorway.

"You don't know what the fuck I'm trying to do, *little boy*." She put emphasis on 'little boy' and slammed my door, walking out the block.

It was shift change, so I wouldn't be able to check her until tomorrow. I laid down in my bed with my thoughts all over the place. I had been doing all this talking shit and bragging, but what if I didn't beat the charges?

Chapter Three

Girl, you can do this—This will get Face out of jail and back to you, she thought to herself.

She had to psych herself up. Taking a life wasn't something you did on an everyday basis, even though she had done it before. She smoked two blunts and downed three shots of gin, yet her nerves were still rattled. She rubbed her hands down the front of the nurse uniform she was wearing, trying to wipe away the sweat that had accumulated on her palms.

She fingered the insulin-filled syringe in her pocket. The syringe felt like a hundred pounds in her pocket. Her mind was telling her that everyone could see it and knew what she was there to do. She felt like the police were going to jump out and arrest her at any moment. Then she would be in the same place as Face, and that wasn't an option. She had big plans for Face. He couldn't do what needed to be done sitting inside of a jail cell; but, with him home, the sky was the limit. Her reign as Queen would be endless. It was amazing the things a woman in love would do for their man. Nothing was off limits—from selling their bodies to committing felonies. She was deeply in love. Besides that, she knew Face was destined for great things. And if she had anything to do with it, she was going to be on his lap as he sat on his throne.

She got off the elevator on the intensive care unit. She checked to make sure her wig was on right, and proceeded down the hall. The overweight cop sitting outside the room at the end of the hallway let her know which one they had Kameesha in. There was no way the fat cop could catch her if things got out of hand.

Why hadn't Kameesha just kept her dick suckers closed? She wouldn't even be in this situation, and her mother and brother would still be alive. But because Kameesha wanted to be a whore and was recorded doing it, then she got put on blast. She got in her feelings. Her brother did what any brother would've done and tried to protect his sister's honor, not knowing that Kameesha didn't own any honor. All shooting Face earned him was a torturous road to meet the creator.

"How are you doing tonight, Ms. Jackson?" the cop questioned, reading the name tag she had stolen.

"Fine. I'm just coming to check her vitals for the night."

She smiled, disappearing into Kameesha's room.

She walked over to the bedside and looked down at the heavily bandaged Kameesha. Ninety-five percent of her body had third-degree burns from Face pouring the scalding hot baby oil on her when he had her tied up. Sensing her presence, Kameesha opened her eyes. Her eyes got huge when she saw who was standing over her. Kameesha knew her time on earth was about to end because tears started to flow from her eyes. She pulled the syringe out and was about to put it into the IV when she heard a male voice.

"It's a shame what that boy did to her. I hope they give him the needle," the guard said, standing in the door.

She tucked the needle and spun around. "Sir, you can't be in here!" she snapped.

He went back to his post, but not before glancing back over his shoulder a last time.

She disconnected the EKG machine so the nurses' station wouldn't be alerted when Kameesha flatlined. She had learned online that if you gave a healthy person insulin, it would send them into a coma and they'd die.

"I'm sorry," she said, emptying the insulin into Kameesha's IV.

She didn't stay around to see the results. She left Kameesha's room and walked briskly down the stairwell. If she survived a syringe filled with insulin, then she deserved to be alive. She tossed the blond wig in the trash, and walked out of the hospital. Now all she had to do was, wait for Face to get out and her reign at the top would begin.

***

It was 6 o'clock on the dot, and I was up waiting on Ms. Gipson to walk in the block. I had to check her big chested ass. She peeked at my room when she walked in. She knew I was about to go in her shit. Ms. Gipson popped the top floor out for their rec and sat down. I pressed the intercom button, and she ignored my shit. She wanted to play games.

"What do you need, Face?"

"Stop playing with me and come here!" I demanded.

She chuckled and turned the intercom off.

That was something I hated about being incarcerated. All the female officers acted as if they were supermodels when they looked more like something from the movie titled *Wrong Turn*. Don't get me wrong; there were some good looking officers, but they weren't many. Then I couldn't really blame them. I needed to blame all the suckers that were locked up and blowing their heads up by telling them how good they looked. That's when a nigga like me brought them down to size.

"Face, you got an attorney visit." Ms. Gipson hit my intercom. I was already dressed. So when she popped my door, I stepped right out.

I went to the desk and said, "You should be glad a nigga of my caliber is even talking to you."

I could tell my statement had caught her off guard, and she didn't know how to respond. She was used to niggas kissing her ass because she wasn't ugly. Ms. Gipson was so put off by me not sucking up to her that she let me slide out the block without shackles.

I hoped my sexy ass lawyer had her shit together today, or she was getting fired on the spot.

"How are you today, Mr. Lowe?" she asked.

Her perfume had the normal sweet smell typical of a woman, its fragrance pervading the air in the room.

"Good as long as you got it together." I grabbed a seat beside her to see if I could rattle her.

I could tell by her look that she wanted to speak on me being so close to her, but she didn't. Instead, she said: "In case you haven't heard, the only living witness in your case passed away last night."

"So why am I still in this orange bodysuit?" I was curious to know.

She laughed, showing me her teeth were perfect.

"When you were arrested, you had a gun on you and the bullets matched those found at a crime scene in Taylor's Creek where two people were shot. I expect you to be charged in the next hour, or they'll have to release you." She closed her briefcase and stood up to leave.

The Fendi business suit she had on looked like someone had painted it on. And I was right about her having a super phat ass. Her waist didn't exist, and that led up to a pair of juicy breasts that I could hear saying: *Come suck me.*

"Oh yea," she leaned down and whispered in my ear, "I don't give a fuck who you think you are but if you ever walk out of a meeting with me involved again, you'll need a new lawyer. And in case you didn't know, I'm the best criminal lawyer on the east coast." And with that she walked out.

I liked her, I thought, walking back to the block. There was a Native American behind the desk, with three stripes on her shoulder indicating that she was a sergeant. She was probably just relieving Ms. Gipson.

"Bro, that bitch searched your room while you were gone with her police ass," Ox informed me.

"Who?"

"That bitch behind the desk." He mean-mugged her.

"Make that your last time calling me a bitch. Come here, Lowe." She motioned.

"What up?" I asked.

"Pocahontas sent you her love. It's under your pillow."

I left and went to my room. I looked under my pillow and there was a phone, an ounce of loud, and a bag of dark liquid that I knew was Hennessy. Pocahontas had come through!

"Ox, come here. Roll some of this up and go get a bottle."

I was up all night, thinking. Not just about his proposition but a scheme I had come up with. While I was out of duty, somebody had beat me to some of the robberies I had planned on executing, taking money out of my mouth. So the question came to me last night: Why didn't I just get all the jackboys in the city to join my team so that way I would get paid regardless?

And the ones that didn't . . . *Bang! Bang!*

"What's the business?" Ox walked back into the room.

I filled his bottle up with the Cognac, and we walked out to the rec yard, which wasn't nothing but four thirty foot walls with a grate over the top.

"Check this, bro. Kameesha died last night, so them murder charges is dead. All I got is some bullshit charges hanging over my head. I want to run something by you real quick because I won't be here in the next four hours."

I took a few pulls of the gas he passed me.

"What if I could get all the jackboys in the city to join me? *Jackboy Mafia*, yea, that got a ring to it."

"Quick question. Why join you when they can keep doing their own thing and not have to split their money more ways? And I'm talking about the heavy hittas! Thrones who hit for hundred racks on the regular." Ox asked a legitimate question, one I had asked myself when I was throwing the idea around in my head.

"Immunity."

Chapter Four

I got released from the county jail a few hours after me and Ox had our talk on the rec yard. I was never charged with the shooting in Taylor's Creek. There was a lack of evidence because no one was willing to testify. No one knew I was getting released, so I called an Uber. I wanted to surprise everybody but first, I had to go check on my investment. A black-on-black Camaro pulled up, and a white dude stuck his head out his window and asked me: "You need an Uber, dude?"

I got in the back seat, only to find two Hispanic chicks already in the back.

"I hope you don't mind, man. You can ride in the front if you want," he said.

I looked the two Spanish girls over, and shook my head. I was straight.

"I'm going to *Pleasure's Paradise*," I said.

The girls giggled. "You too. We're trying to get a job there."

"A job doing what?" They weren't working with a thing in the body department, but their faces were top-notch.

"Either bottle girls or bartenders," the girls chorused.

The driver said: "Man, *Pleasure's Paradise* has become the go-to spot. Overnight, I make so much money taking and picking people up from the club that all I have to do is sit in the parking lot."

"Before you two leave tonight, give me your applications personally and I'll see about getting you two hired."

If the club was doing this good, then my pockets should be doing even better. Hopefully, Pocahontas valued her life more than a few coins because if my paper wasn't correct, she was gonna be on the front page.

We pulled into the parking lot of *Pleasure's Paradise*, and there wasn't an empty spot in sight. And it was only Wednesday! The line was at least forty people long. This was my spot, so I definitely wasn't gonna wait in no line. I walked up to the door, and didn't recognize either of the two burly bouncers.

"What's it gonna cost me because I ain't waiting in no line."

I took the modest approach instead of just walking in.

"You don't look like you belong in here, homie, why don't you got to Secrets or Sharkys?" one said, earning him his first strike.

"You got it big, homie."

"I been had it, now take your bum ass to the back of the line," he said; that made strike two.

This was unacceptable! Not only was he telling potential customers to go to a different strip club, but he was also disrespecting them. I was a street nigga, but I still knew the do's and don'ts when it came to business. Furthermore, had I not had a stake in the club, I would be getting ready to shoot the motherfucker up and ruin everybody's night.

"If you knew who I was, your mouth wouldn't be so reckless. Disrespect another one of my customers, and this will be your last night working here."

"Do you hear this nigga? You're off your rocker but I'm about to beat some sense into you!" He started walking my way.

"Big Mike, if you put your hands on that one, they're gonna be calling your next of kin to identify your body," a golden-brown beauty said from the line.

Her comment made him pause. I closed the distance between us with three quick steps, and tried to put my fist through his throat. He buckled to his knees where I put a knee to his temple, knocking him out.

The scene drew a large crowd, bringing Pocahontas out to see what was going on. Her jaw fell to the floor when she saw me.

"When did you get out? Wait, you didn't escape, did you?" she asked, then saw that I was standing over one of the bouncers.

"What the hell is going on?" she questioned.

I walked past her into the strip club. She could deal with the bouncer situation. I had some bread to check on. The minute the girls saw me, they all rushed up to me, hugging and kissing me.

"I don't know where y'all lips have been, so keep them off of me." I smiled, but was dead ass serious.

I looked around and it was lit! There wasn't a spot on the floor that didn't have money on it. It was obvious that wet and wild Wednesday was a hit. The girls inside the pool were cutting a fool! One was doing a hand stand while the other one was twerking on top of her. Through it all, all my eyes saw were dollar signs. And pussy, of course. I listened to the girls tell me how much they missed me, all the while continuing to check out the club. My baby had been right, this shit was a hit. I only wished she was here to see it. I chilled long enough for Pocahontas to deal with the bouncer and come in. She pulled me away from the girls, leading me up to my office. I took a seat at my desk in the black high- backed chair, and stared at Pocahontas. She had on a red G-string with a red bra under this black fishnet body suit.

"Why are you dressed like that?" I wondered.

"I still dance, I told you that." She opened the wall safe behind the Scarface picture to my right.

Pocahontas started pulling bundles of cash from the titanium safe, sitting them on the massive mahogany desk I was sitting behind.

"This is what we made in two days of being open. Can you imagine what the weekend is gonna look like?" She grinned like a kid on Christmas morning.

"How much is this?"

"Eighty-five racks! And you need to give the bottle girls and bartenders a raise because most of this money came from liquor sales."

Pocahontas explained further. "Here," she said after her explanation, handing me the balance sheet and all the other paperwork that I either needed to look over or sign. I would do all that later. Her giving them to me let me know that she had done her job, and that all the numbers were going to add up.

"So are you gonna keep me as manager or nah?" she asked

"Do you want to stay on?" I moved to the one-way mirrors surrounding the office so I could look out over the club.

"Yes!"

"That's that, now come here real quick. Do you know this girl?"

I pointed at the golden-brown chick who tried to come to my rescue outside.

"No, do I need to get her put out?"

"Nah, she good."

"Okay. It's almost time for me to go on stage, I'll be back." She walked to the door, then looked back over her shoulder. "You still never told me how you got out."

I smiled. "Later. Now go get that paper."

She closed the door there and then.

I turned on the 60-inch flatscreen, and they were playing one of my favorite movies—*Belly*.

This was probably going to be one of the only times I was going to have some down time. I planned on putting my plan in motion asap. You couldn't tell me I wasn't going to see one hundred million before I turned 21.

"Ohh shit, Bunz! You were onto something," I said out loud. Watching them count the money from robbing the club gave me a hell of an idea. I looked at the piles of money in front of me, and the jackboy in me reared its head. What if I could rob all the clubs in the city? Better yet, what if I could own all the high-end strip clubs in the city? I had to find a way to work that into my plan, own all the local high-end strip clubs—by choice or by force.

Chapter Five

I slept at the club my first night home. I wasn't ready to deal with everyone else's emotions at the moment. I knew my mother was gonna be emotional. My cougar—Angie—was, too. Then seeing Chell and my son was going to present a whole 'nother situation in itself. Who knows how I was going to react, being able to hold my son for the first time! So all that was being put on hold, but I did have to call Murph. I need a hammer. It was time to get active.

I sat up on the pink couch in my office, and rubbed the sleep out my eyes. I looked and saw I hadn't put the money back in the safe. We had added another fifteen racks to the money after closing the club. That upped the take to a hundred racks in three days. After paying taxes and the payroll, I was probably going to make a $65,000 profit. How could I complain? Pocahontas warned me that the money wasn't always this good. She explained that we were the hot new club at the moment, and we needed to ride the wave while it was hot. Little did she know I planned on keeping *Pleasure's Paradise* the hot new thing. I wanted to make *Pleasure's Paradise* the hottest strip club on the east coast. I put on my clothes and started putting the money in the wall safe. I was still in the same clothes from Cynthia's funeral: some black Kobe 11's. And I wasn't going to change, I was thugging! It wasn't a real street nigga alive that hadn't worn the same outfit two days in a row. I was dressed appropriately to put part one of my plan in motion. Me and Ox had agreed that I was going to take control of his gang of terrorists because it looked like he was going to be incarcerated for a long time. I had agreed, but what Ox didn't know was that I had absolutely no plans on leaving him behind the wall. I was going to do everything humanly possible to get him out. I looked at the security monitors and saw Murph get out of a red Impala on 28's. I closed the safe, and put the Scarface picture back on the wall.

"I'm on the way out," I called Murph and told him.

I walked out the club into the blistering summer heat. There was a slight breeze, but it did nothing to alleviate the sun's bright rays. My long sleeve button-up was sticking to me, and I hadn't been outside five minutes.

"How it feel to be free?" Murph gave me a half hug, passed me a kush-filled blunt and a high point 9mm.

"It seems like you want me to go from jail to the grave. What am I supposed to do with this? You know they be jamming up."

I turned the bulky gun over in my hand.

"I guess you want mine then." He showed me a Taurus 45.

I reached for it, and Murph said: "Yea right," pulling it back. I got in the Impala, shaking my head.

"So where are we going? And why you ain't called Angie worrisome ass yet? She blowing up everybody else phone trying to get at you."

I shrugged.

"Laci and Rai'chell said fuck you too," Murph informed me.

"They'll be okay, I'm taking care of business. And we're going to Cliffdale Forest. Unfortunately, there's a couple there that doesn't believe in keeping their mouths closed. So, we're going to pay them a house call." I pulled on the blunt and lost all my breath.

I started beating on my chest, trying to get my breath back while Murph laughed so hard he was crying. I got my breath back, and was higher than high. I wasn't used to blowing on big blunts after being in the county jail.

"You higher than a kite," he grinned, looking over at me.

"A kite? My nigga, kites don't get this high." I leaned my seat back, enjoying my high.

Murph chuckled and turned on the new Lil Baby mixtape

The couple stayed on the first street in Cliffdale Forest. We were lucky to find them in their front yard. I knew my task wasn't going to be hard after seeing the couple. They looked to be in their mid-sixties. Murph parked in front of their house, and I hopped out. The couple watched me as I approached them.

"Look, y'all don't know me but you can consider me the quiet before the storm."

"What are you talking about, young man?" the elderly man questioned.

"Someone tried to rob you a while ago. All I need you to do is tell the police that they have the wrong person."

"No! He deserves to be in prison!" he yelled.

"Calm down, Harold." His wife placed her hand on his arm.

"Get out of my yard! Now! He pulled a .38 special out and pointed it in my direction.

I looked to the skies. I didn't understand how I was always the one finding myself in the dumbest of situations. None of my niggas had this problem. *Boom! Boom!* I looked, and the old man's head was gone! His wife screamed as his body fell to the ground. I put two slugs in her chest, sending her to the Pearly Gates with her dearly beloved.

"Nigga, you coulda shot me!" I got back in the car, looking at Murph.

"Better me than him. How would it look for a gangsta to get killed by a senior citizen?"

"You got issues." I laughed. "Take me by that lawyer's office.

While Murph drove us downtown, I filled him in on my plans with starting *Jackboy Mafia* and adding Ox's *Turban Gang* into the fold.

"I'm feeling that because we can't be everywhere at once," Murph said.

"And fuck making Ross king of 301, that's thinking too small. What if our nigga was king of the city?" The idea popped into my head.

"Bro, I'm with whatever. As long as my pockets are heavy, I could care less."

"Say no more."

We pulled into the high-rise that Ms. Whitlock's office was located in, and I got out. Everywhere I looked, there were foreign cars. From Maserati's to Porsche's. What I didn't know was that the building housed other lawyers, state prosecutors, as well as federal prosecutors. I walked inside the building, and asked the receptionist what floor Ms. Whitlock's office was on.

"Thirteen," she informed me, never taking her eyes off the *US Weekly* magazine.

I got on the elevator. I was the only person in street clothes; everyone else was in business attire. I got off on the thirteenth floor, and was relieved that there weren't many people in the waiting area.

"Is Ms. Whitlock in?" I asked the secretary.

"Do you have an appointment, sir?"

"No, but I'm sure she will find a way to fit me into her schedule. Tell her Mr. Lowe is here."

She grabbed the phone to call Ms. Whitlock. After a brief conversation, the secretary said: "Ms. Whitlock said she won't be able to see you today, her schedule is full."

I looked around the waiting area and counted five people. The law firm was called *Whitlock and Associates*, so there was no way everybody was there to see her.

"How many of y'all are here to see Ms. Whitlock?" I grilled the room, and only one person raised a hand.

Oh, she had me fucked up! I got up and walked into the back. I had no clue where I was headed. I made a right, and walked down the hallway.

"Sir, you really can't be back here, you're going to get me fired." The secretary's plea fell on deaf ears.

I was unsympathetic to her pleas. I had chosen the right path after all. It turned out that the end of the hallway sat Ms. Whitlock's office. I knew this because the closed door advertised it.

"She's in an important meeting," the secretary continued to beg behind me.

I walked in, and found her in a meeting with four other people, one of them being detective Corrigan!

Nicholas Lock

Chapter Six

Me and detective Corrigan had history. He was my plug on all the D-boys. If they refused to pay him, he would allow us to rob them with no consequence. I hadn't seen him since before I had gotten shot.

"I'm sorry, Ms. Whitlock. He wouldn't listen, do you want me to call security?"

"No. Jamie, that won't be necessary." Ms. Whitlock stood up. "Gentleman, I think that'll be all. Bobby, my client isn't taking anything over seven years." She addressed the other male in the room.

"Tasha, you better talk some sense into him then because I'm not going any lower than twelve," the white man in the grey suit—whom I assumed was a prosecutor—said.

"Trial it is," the fourth person in the room said, who happened to be a dark-skinned female in a blue Gucci pantsuit.

The prosecutor shrugged and walked out with Corrigan in tow.

"Amanda, I'll get with you in a minute," Ms. Whitlock said, ushered the dark-skinned lady out the room, and closed the door.

"You have a lot of nerve barging into my office like you own it!" She walked back behind the cherry wood desk, standing in front of the floor-to-ceiling window. "I told you before—"

As she stood in front of the window, she didn't realize that the sun was shining straight through the yellow sundress she was wearing, giving me a clear view of her womanly shape.

"It's no way you wore that to court today," I cut her off.

"I didn't have court today. What makes you say that and are you not listening to anything I said." She turned around, giving me a better view.

I felt like a pervert, so I diverted my attention to the degrees decorating her walls.

"I don't listen to my mom when she chastises me, so you're wasting precious breath. I say that because first off, that dress is too tight. Secondly, I can see through it."

She moved away from the window.

"You're a mannish little boy." Ms Whitlock folded her arms across her chest, and leaned against a bookcase.

"Lady, I ain't been a little boy since I was about thirteen so it'd be in your best interest to remember that the next time you address me. Now I came here to talk business. I don't want to hear all that other frivolous talk because it's going to get us nowhere." I leaned back in the chair I was in, and stared at her.

She matched my stare with a raised brow. I could tell she was used to being the dominant person in the situation. If my plan was going to work, I was going to need her if she was as good as she said she was. So, I was going to let her have this battle for the moment. I was trying to win the war.

"Okay, lady, you got it. I need you. You said you were the best lawyer on the east coast. It's time for you to prove it."

"How is that?"

"I need my homeboy out of jail. He was accused of shooting a police officer and killing one, but witnesses are deceased." I gave her the details.

"What about the cop that's alive?"

"Doesn't remember what the suspect looks like."

"I'll have him out in a month." She spoke confidently, looking for a pen to write down the name. "Next time, make an appointment. You can't be busting into my office like that. Courtesy demands that you—"

I was already gone, slamming the door to her office before she finished.

"You ready to put that work in?" Corrigan asked me when I came out of the building.

He was leaning against the wall, smoking a Newport short.

"I was ready when I got out of the hospital, but you was bullshitting. You got a folder for me now? I was eager to see the *Turban Gang* cut up."

Every time Corrigan had a D-boy for me to hit, it always came in a folder with a picture and a brief story on them. See, the only D-boys we were supposed to hit were the ones that refused to pay Corrigan to sell drugs. But you know we were still gonna be hitting niggas.

"No, but I'll have one for you in a few days," he said, as Murph pulled up.

He walked off, and I got in the whip with Murph.

"What he speaking about?" Murph asked.

"Getting to the bag as usual. He gon' have a folder for us in a few days. I gotta go by Rai'chell's and Angie's. You can drop me off at the spot."

I was about to hit the shower and change clothes. I had been in the same ones for the last few days; I was pushing it.

"Good because I got a hot date." Murph licked his lips.

"Tell Vanessa I said hi."

"Vanessa is old news. I got a new bitch!"

"Who? Better yet, I don't even want to know." I turned the Lil Baby up, and sparked the roach up that was in the ashtray.

Being that we were downtown, it didn't take us long to reach the split level we were renting across the river. The roach had me moving in slow motion. I got out, and Murph peeled out. I went in, going straight to my safe. I pulled $15,000 out, and closed it back. I kept some money here, but my real stash was at Angie' house. I took a long, hot shower, and got myself ready to deal with a mad Angie and a furious Rai'chell. They both had been blowing my phone up, but I was ignoring them. We were going to be face to face soon. I put on a pair of Burberry shorts and a white t-shirt with some white low top 1's. Other than my earrings, the only other jewelry I wore was the 9mm Ruger tucked in my waistline. I hopped in my white Cadillac truck and rode out. I was gonna holler at Rai'chell first since she had my son. I called her, and she answered with an attitude.

"What?"

"Cut it out. I hear you smiling through the phone. You at your mom's?" I asked.

"No, I'm at my place."

"Your place?"

"I told you a lot has changed. I got a place in Odom Townhouses." She shocked me.

"Be outside, I'll be pulling up in about ten minutes." I ended the call.

How had her seventeen-year-old ass got an apartment? I was about to find that out and more. I pulled into the townhouses, and she was outside sitting on the hood of a purple Challenger on 24's.

"Get off them people car before I have to fuck somebody up, and why you got them little ass shorts on? Where the rest of your clothes at?"

Rai'chell had on some white itty bitty shorts that had her pussy poking out and the bottom of her ass saying hello. Then she had on a half shirt that showed the bottom of her plump breasts. I wasn't gon' lie: she was looking like new money. Rai'chell's cinnamon-brown skin was glowing, and her freckles added to her sex appeal. My baby had turned into a woman.

"Nigga, this my shit." She took her time getting off the car so I could get a good look at her features. "Come on, so you can meet your son."

I followed her inside her spot, and was impressed. The tan and white color scheme gave the living room a homey feel. And the jasmine candles had it smelling good. I saw my son in his playpen asleep with his butt in the air. I grabbed him and sat on the tan leather loveseat.

"Hey, man!" I tried waking him up.

"If you wake him, you gon' be the one to put him back to sleep." Rai'chell sat beside me on the loveseat, curling her legs under her.

"I got this." I laid him across my lap. "Now who got you that car and this spot?" I grilled her.

She smiled before saying "You, nigga! I saved a majority of that money you used to give me. So I was able to get the Challenger, and my mom signed for the townhouse"

She eased my mind. "What's going on with this head?" Rai'chell ran her hand through my afro.

Everyone was used to seeing me with a low cut.

"I don't know, I'm thinking about growing it out." I eyed the phat print between her legs.

"Nymel, are you my man or what?" She caught me off guard.

"Something like that." I grinned and she mushed me.

"For real, Nymel, I don't have time for the games. What is it gonna be? I want us to be a family. I have your only child. That should mean something to you."

"It does, Chell. I just don't know how all of this is gonna fit into my immediate plans."

"Just tell me we're exclusive, and we'll deal with all the minor stuff as it comes."

"Exclusive?"

"I'm your only girl, no one is gonna pop up pregnant anymore." She put her white tipped finger in my face.

"Okay, Chell, okay, I got you." I gave in.

"That was really your only choice because if you would've said no, I was gonna kill you." She produced a 9mm out of the couch.

Before I could say anything, she said: "Now come on. It's been a long time since you fucked your pussy."

"You was playing about killing me though, right?" I asked, carrying Nymel Junior behind her up the stairs.

Chapter Seven

The constant ringing of my phone woke me up out of the deep slumber I was in. I looked to my left and saw Chell and my baby boy both fast asleep. Me and Chell had went at it in the bed the way we used to, but with an added energy and intensity making for a mind-numbing first round. The second round was strictly lovemaking as per her request. It was slow and sensual. Afterwards, we tried to go to sleep but my son had other plans. He woke up in his crib, hungry, and made sure to tell us about it. Even after Nymel Junior got fed, he stayed up. I wasn't able to drift off to sleep until 1 o'clock in the morning. Now it was three a.m., and I was getting woke back up. I grabbed my phone and saw it was my twin calling. I knew he was about to go in his bag. I hadn't called him since I had gotten out of jail, so I could imagine he was mad.

"Yo," I answered softly, trying not to wake Chell or my son up.

"You a mack! You ain't called me one time to let me know you was out. I had to find out through Murph!"

"Bro, it's so much shit going on. I ain't had a chance to really sit down. I been on go mode. I'm trying to set some shit in motion, and it's consuming all my time. I ain't even talked to mama. But before the week is out, I'm gon' touch base with everyone." I reassured him, easing out of the bed.

"Don't worry because I'm coming down there."

Trip was the starting quarterback at UNC. As a freshman, he led UNC to their first national championship and won the Heisman trophy. Draft experts were projecting Trip to go number one in the NFL draft. And the team they were projecting him to go to was my favorite team—the Carolina Panthers.

"Bro, don't come down here. I'll come to you. Shit is about to hit the fan. We gon' really turn Fayetteville into

45

Fayettenam. It's gon' be a war zone, and I don't need you getting caught in the mix."

"Well, you got two days or I'm coming down there!" he warned.

"Yea, yea, nigga. Love you, bro." I ended the call.

I was standing in the window, looking out at the starless night sky, when my phone rang again. I looked and saw it was Angie. I had forgot to call her. I looked back at Rai'chell, and she was staring at me.

"Answer it!" she dared.

"It's Angie, girl, go back to sleep," I told her. "What up, sugar mama?" I answered.

"Since I'm not important enough to receive a phone call, I'd like for you to come get your clothes and money!" Her voice trembled.

"I'm on the way." I ended the call.

I started putting my clothes on. I had to go pacify my cougar. There wasn't a chance in hell I was gonna let her end our situationship. She was more than just a chick I fucked. I had genuine love for Angie. We had major history.

"Is she okay?" Chell leaned up on her elbow.

"She's good," I said, putting my sneakers on.

Rai'chell wouldn't have been so understanding if she knew the extent of me and Angie's relationship. Rai'chell knew we had love for each other, but she was under the assumption that it was a platonic love, a motherly love with Angie being forty-two years old. If only she knew! The things we did, a mother and son should never even think about doing.

I kissed Chell and my son, and went to fix shit with Angie. I knew I wasn't shit. I had told Rai'chell a few hours ago that we were exclusive. Then again, her *exclusive* meant she was my only girl; and technically, she was. I didn't know him, but

I always heard my daddy wasn't shit. I guess I'm a chip off the old block.

I got in my truck and bee-lined it to Angie's house. I let myself in, and found Angie sitting on the sofa in her silk nightgown. She was sipping on a glass of white wine. She didn't look up from the reality show she was watching.

"Baby, I know you're not gon' act like that." I got down on the floor between her legs.

She continued to ignore my presence.

"So what? You don't love me no more?" I asked.

My question made her look at me for a brief second before focusing back on the *Basketball Wives*.

"Baby, say something. I can't take you not talking to me."

"Really? Because it seems like you were doing just fine and dandy until I told you to come get your stuff," Angie said, continuing to watch TV.

Since I was already between her legs, all I had to do was lean forward and I was face to face with her coochie. Angie didn't have any panties on beneath her nightgown. She tried to push my head from between her thick thighs, but my lips latched onto her clit.

"Ssss!" She hissed, rocking her hips.

I sucked her clit into my warm mouth, and Angie went from pushing my head to pulling my hair.

"Nooooo, Face. Don't do me like this!" She moaned.

I put Angie's legs over my shoulders and ate my late night snack.

I spelled *I love you* on her clit, and got rewarded with a mouthful of her love potion. Angie expected me to put her leg down. Instead, I pushed them up higher, forcing her to lean back. I pulled my swollen manhood out before Angie had time to react, and invaded her warm velvety walls.

"Oh Gawd! You feel sooo good!" Angie dug her nails into my forearms.

With every plunge into Angie's wet pussy, I pulled her to me by the hips. Wet, squishy sounds resounded from her love tunnel; that was turning me on even more.

"Turn over," I said, breathing hard.

Angie turned around, and bent over the seat of the sofa. I slid inside her from the back. She was so wet and tight. She moaned as I inched inside her. I went in deeper and deeper until I had given her my all, then I began to stroke her nice and long.

"I'm about to cum, oh my God! I'm about to cum so hard! Fuck me like only you can, Face!" Angie squeezed her pussy as tight as she could around my dick.

"Oh shit! Oh shit! Boy, you're fucking the shit out of me." Angie's eyes rolled to the back of her head as she bit down on her bottom lip.

Angie's first orgasm caused her whole body to shake.

Looking down at Angie's pretty caramel ass, I smacked it hard.

"Ssss!" Angie hissed. "Do that again. Yesss. I like that."

I reached out and pinched her nipples. Angie came again, moaning from deep within her soul. I enjoyed her climax as much as she did.

"I'm about to cum, Angie!" I grunted, as I began to fuck her with urgency.

"Oh yea, just like that. Fuck me harder. Make it hurt, Face!"

I closed my eyes, gritted my teeth, gripped Angie's hips firmly, and came with such force I thought my kids might come out of her mouth.

Breathing hard, we both slowed down. I pulled out and lay back on the soft carpet, trying to catch my breath.

"You're not getting off the hook that easy." Angie stood over me.

"Come on, boo, you know how I'm living. I been going one hundred mph ever since I got out. You know where we stand at." I was still trying to catch my breath. "No one will ever take your place, Angie, that shit is wrote in blood. We have a special kind of love. You think I'd let you hold the majority of my money if you weren't important?" I broke it down to her.

"Now that you break it down like that, I understand. I'm sorry for riding you like that. Even though we're no longer in a relationship, I still be feeling like it."

"It's all good. Just get down here and ride me the way you're supposed to."

"You ain't said nothing." Angie sat on my dick and rode me until the sun started to peek over the horizon.

Nicholas Lock

Chapter Eight

I let my vision for my plan take me off balance. I had almost forgot about Rude Boy's treachery. I was directing my resources elsewhere when it should have been on putting Rude Boy in the dirt, but I was about to fix that. Rude Boy was in the county jail on a dope charge. He had sold eighteen ounces to a confidential informant. At the moment, his bond was a quarter million dollars. That was why me and Murph were at Q's bail bonds office. I was going to bond Rude Boy out just so I could smoke his ass. We had a dope fiend sign the papers so we wouldn't be connected in any way. We dropped the fiend off, and grabbed something to eat from Wendy's. I ordered the classic double and told them to biggie-size it, while Murph ordered a salad.

"A salad?" I looked over at Murph.

"I'm trying to lose this weight. I'm not playing football anymore, so it's no need for me to be this heavy."

Me, my twin and Murph all stood 6'0, but Murph played on the defensive line so he needed to be heavier than us. He tipped the scale at three hundred pounds but moved like he was half that size. Murph got offers from all the D-1 schools to come play, and he was only a junior. But like me, he had fell out of love with the game and fell head over heels in love with the streets. Personally, I would have preferred he went off to college like Trip, but how could I tell my day one not to play the streets when I was! Plus I knew without a doubt that he was one of the select few I could trust to watch my back.

"I'm telling you, bro, we about to be all the way up! The only thing that can stop us is us!" I stated.

Truth be told, we were already up. The last lick we had hit put us over the million mark, and I was only eighteen while Murph was seventeen. Most people would have stopped, but then what were we to do? Bill Gates and Jeff Bezos reached the billion dollar mark, and they kept going. I didn't hear anybody telling them they had enough money. Even Mark Cuban, the owner of the Dallas Mavericks, said he was trying to be a trillionaire!

"I'm with it. And I found a legit little hustle that keeps them people off my back. I be flipping cars. I'm gon' get my dealer's license and open a car dealership!" Murph informed me.

"You should open an exotic car dealership, that'll bring in the big bag." I gave my opinion.

We got the food and headed back downtown. I wasn't trying to miss Rude Boy. I parked at the launderette across the street from the jail, and waited. We finished our food, as they started the afternoon visits. The old Pastor Troy bumping out of the speakers of the '05 Caprice had us bopping our heads. We were ready to take Rude Boy out the game once and for all. The new AR-15 between my legs was dying to spit, and Murph had a AK-56. Death was around the corner and coming fast.

"There he go right there!" Murph pointed.

We pulled our masks down, then I pulled out of the launderette and sat in the median in front of the jail. *Kah! Kah! Kah!* I got out of the car, letting the AR talk! Murph did the same thing. Everybody going in the jail for visitation scattered, giving me a clear shot at Rude Boy. *Kah! Kah! Kah!* I let off a quick burst, hitting him in the chest. Rude Boy crumpled to the ground, giving me a sense of satisfaction. We got back in the car, did 100mph past the market house, up Ramsey Street, past the social service building all the way to Elliott Circle. I pulled into the projects, and we got out.

"Boy, I hit a few of them civilians." Murph looked at me over the roof of the car.

"Casualties of war." I shrugged and got in the rental car I had parked in the projects earlier.

We drove back the way we came. I expected to see a white outline, but all I saw were a bunch of patrol cars. I kept going straight ahead. We were on our way to Taylor's Creek. With their leader incarcerated, the dudes loyal to Rude Boy's cause folded when Ross came through. Now my nigga controlled the entire section of 301 that ran through Fayetteville.

"Wait until you see this nigga," Murph grinned. I made the left inside Taylor's Creek, and drove to the back. It was deep as hell outside. It looked like the club had just let out, and this was the after-party spot. Niggas was dripped up, and the hoes had on the least amount of clothes possible without being naked. I wasn't able to drive all the way through because the street was so packed with people. Soon as I parked and got out, Ross materialized out of nowhere and picked me up.

"Goddamn boy! I knew your ass was going to come check your boy out sooner or later." He put me down.

"Oh shit! Bitch, you dripped all the way up!" I checked Ross out.

His 5'9 frame was dripped head to toe in Prada. He had so many Cuban links around his neck, it was crazy. The diamonds in his ears made mine look like grains of sand. Then the Hublot Big Bang watch Ross was wearing had so many diamonds in it you couldn't even tell what time it was.

"I stumbled up on a plug on that dog food, and I ain't looked back," he told me, leading me to a white Porsche 911 Carrera S.

I turned to look for Murph, and he was whispering in the ear of a chocolate stallion in a pink and black mini.

"I'm glad you said that because I'm on some shit like fuck 301, why not the whole city?" I grabbed a seat inside the Porsche.

"My thoughts exactly but I need your help. Yea, I got plenty of soldiers but that's because I'm keeping them fed. So they're only loyal to the dead presidents I help them get. If I was to fall off right now, more than half of them would find the next nigga on the come up and join his team. But you—" he looked at me. "You really want to see your nigga on top. Not once through this whole ordeal have you asked me for one red penny. That's how I know your intentions are legit and it's also why this Porsche is yours." He smiled.

"What?"

"Yea, this you, bro. It's a small price to pay. It's rare today to find niggas as loyal as you are. You're the last of a dying breed. Most dudes are so money-motivated nowadays that they'll give up their own flesh and blood for the almighty dollar."

"Blood makes us related but loyalty makes us family," I said.

"Facts. Now come on, let's enjoy this party."

I didn't leave Taylor's Creek until two in the morning, in my new Porsche of course. Before I got home, Ox hit me up with the cellphone I had left him.

"What up, homie? Did you get that?" I inquired.

I had sent him some more loud and some Newports through Pocahontas' homegirl.

"Yea, good looking out but bro, that nigga got clapped coming out of the county today but he lived."

"A'ight, thanks for letting me know." I ended the call.

The nigga Rude Boy was like project roaches, they were hard to kill. A headshot was in his future.

Chapter Nine

"Tali! Tali! Tali! Turban gang! Terrorist gang! Tiara gang! TNT!" They chanted on and on.

Me and Murph were at Seabrook Park on the basketball court with the whole *Turban Gang*. I was meeting them for the first time. There were fifty of them, with ten of them being girls. I tell you, their energy was addictive. It seemed like all they wanted to do was turn up. I was checking all of them out, particularly the females.

It took a different type of chick to really be with the shits and not fold. I was always skeptical when it came to a female being in the streets. Not the streets per se because there's plenty of chicks in the streets, but a chick on that shoot 'em up *bang bang* shit—I didn't feel like they were going to give it their all. And what I had planned was going to require them to give it their all or get out.

There was this one chick in particular that my eyes kept coming back to. While everyone else was chanting, she was quiet, moving through the crowd. Her movements reminded me of a panther on the hunt. She was the shortest person at the park; she was about 3'8 max. She wasn't the only person my eyes lingered on. It was a boy in the group that you couldn't tell me wasn't in elementary school, but he was one of the livest people out there. The only person shorter than him was the quiet girl. The more I looked, the similar the two looked. They were both extremely dark with high cheekbones, full lips and deep-set eyes.

"Okay, okay." Soldier got everyone settled down.

Soldier was who Ox had put in charge while he was in the county. He was a seventeen-year-old hard head from down-town, and Ox's first cousin.

"We need to hear these dudes out. Ox said whatever Scarface says do needs to be done, no questions asked." He called me by my full street name.

"Look, I have a plan that's gonna put major money in all our pockets and y'all will be doing what y'all love to do—terrorize shit. But I need the shit to be done right and I'm sure y'all don't need any lessons in how to terrorize."

"That's an almanac fact!" somebody yelled.

"First thing I need though is to know your names and how old you are."

"Damn, what is this? A job interview?" a girl blurted out, earning her my attention.

She was brown-skinned, tall, and skinny, with short hair. I'd say she was about fourteen. I walked towards her as if I was going to do something to her but before I could get to her, the short quiet girl I had been watching stepped in my path, shaking her head. I tried to step around her, but she got back in my way. I could easily move her tiny frame out my way, but something told me that wouldn't be a wise decision.

"I'm not about to do anything to her. I just want to look her in the eyes while we talk." I reassured the quiet girl.

She looked me over, then let me by.

"What were you saying now?" I invaded her space.

"I didn't come here to be interviewed," she said defiantly.

"That's too bad because you are! Now if you have an issue with any of this, you can bounce!" I got in her face, testing her mettle.

"Get da fuck out my face!" She tried pushing me, but I didn't budge. Then she made the mistake of slapping me. Before I realized it, I had her in the air by her throat.

"You got me fucked up, little girl!" I choked her.

"You only have three seconds to put her down, or you'll die where you stand," an angelic voice said.

I looked for the source of the voice, and felt a tug on my pants leg. I looked down into the purple eyes of the little girl.

"Please don't make me kill you," she said calmly.

It was something about the calm way she said it that made me drop the girl. She fell to her knees, gasping for air. The little girl kicked the girl I was choking in the side.

"Ox said to follow his lead and that's what it is. If he asks you to bend over backwards, you do it." She never raised her voice as she spoke to the girl I had choked.

"Okay, Oshun!" the girl getting kicked yelled.

"I'm talking to the Tiaras of course," Oshun said.

She had the sweetest voice I'd ever heard.

"How old are you?" I wanted to know.

"Sixteen," she replied, catching me off guard. "I'm a dwarf," she added, sensing that I didn't believe her.

"And I'm her brother—Ogun! I'm thirteen," said the boy that I assumed was in elementary school.

They all started saying their names and ages. Their ages ranged from eleven to seventeen. The name of the girl that had stopped me was Tonya, and she was seventeen. She mugged me the entire time that I got her rebuked by Oshun. "Once you and Tonya fight and you win, she'll be one of your most loyal supporters," Menace whispered to me. Endowed with a stocky build and blue eyes, he was fourteen, black like Akon, with dreadlocks hanging down his shoulders.

"What's the deal with Oshun and Ogun?" Murph wondered.

Wolf answered: "Oshun really runs the Tiara gang. They wear Tiaras while we were Turbans. When we yell *TNT*, that means Turbans and Tiaras. Oshun and Ogun are siblings."

Wolf was sixteen, white and slim, with plaits down his back. He was the only white dude in the group.

Wolf added: "If Oshun talks, that usually means she's mad. She rarely talks, so if you hear her voice, something is going on."

"And Ogun is a classic terrorizer, a wild child—His sister is the only one who can control him," Menace said.

"Control him? He's a little boy." Murph laughed.

"Y'all need to get the hell off the court," a dude said, walking up with twenty other dudes.

"You're about to see what we mean right now," Wolf said, walking in the direction of his gang.

Tonya wasted no time taking off! There wasn't any back and forth. She slapped the dude across the face, and stood in the middle of the group of niggas. The dude drew back to hit her, and *splat*! A glob of blood hit the court. Everyone thought she had stopped him, but she had really cut his face open with the razor she had in her hand. The TNT gang circled them, then rushed them. They didn't stand a chance, they were outnumbered and most of the girls were swinging some type of weapon—whether it be a razor or brass knuckles. I could see why they were so feared; they were relentless in their attack. They were like a school of organized piranha. Oshun wasn't participating, though. She was standing by me and Murph. Brandishing two knives with S-shaped blades, Ogun was running through the crowd of people.

One of the dudes managed to pull a gun, and was about to shoot Tonya in the face. I was pulling my fire when a knife appeared in the dude's throat. A blur to my right caught my attention, then another knife appeared in his forehead. I looked as Oshun threw another knife, hitting him in the eye. I had seen enough. They were going to serve my purpose just right. Me and Murph pulled out of Seabrook as Ogun tore a dude's throat out with one of his wicked looking knives.

I was at the house holding my son when Ox called me.

"I heard you seen my gang in action," he bragged.

"Hell yea. That shit made the news, five niggas died. I got to get them some guns though, that knife shit outdated."

"Good luck getting Oshun and Ogun to use them. I heard you and Tonya had a run-in too." Ox laughed.

"Glad that shit tickled you. You better be glad I ain't kill her ass."

"Bro, that wouldn't have gone well. Oshun is very protective over her Tiaras. Beat her ass a little bit, and she'll respect you. Yani is going to probably try you too. Something else I forgot to mention. The way I run the gang is that since you're the alpha, anyone can try you for that spot at any time."

"I'm gonna feel sorry for whoever does," I said, wondering what the hell Ox had got me into.

"Be safe, bro." He ended the call, and I went to put my son in his crib so me and Chell could work on making him a sister.

Chapter Ten

One thing I learned from being in the streets was that you could recognize a nigga for what they were. For instance, I could spot a real hustler on sight. When I say *real*, I'm not talking about the ones who hustle for clothes and jewels. I'm talking about those who trap to get rich like Ross, for instance. But I could spot jackboys even faster, probably because I was a jackboy myself and I knew the mannerisms. And at the moment, I was watching a jackboy by the name of Maino. He was from the eastside of the city. I had been hearing Maino's name, but didn't know what he looked like until now. He was 5'9, dark-skinned, about 180 pounds, and rocked a Caesar. Maino was going to be the first jackboy that I was going to try and recruit. I chose him first because he didn't have a crew, and the word in the streets was that he was downright ruthless. But it was also said that he was a real nigga. Hopefully, he made the right decision because I had Menace and Wolf with me.

We were in the VIP section in the *Pearl Necklace*, a strip club I have my sights on in the city. I was trying to kill two birds with one stone. I was going to try and get Maino to join Jackboy Mafia, and I was about to see if the owner of the *Pearl Necklace* was going to sign his club over. I got up off the couch in VIP and made my way over to where Maino was getting a lap dance, with Menace and Wolf behind me.

"Ma, let me holler at my man real quick," I told the stallion in Maino's lap.

At first, she only looked at us, obviously mad that we were interrupting her cash flow; but when she saw the looks on Menace and Wolf's faces, she got her things and strutted away. The whole time, Maino was just looking at us with a nonchalant look, like he didn't have a worry in the world.

"My G, you better have a real good reason for interrupting my show," Maino stated, pulling a Newport short out.

"I would think so." I took a seat across from him. "I'm gon' cut straight to the chase. I need you on my team, Maino. I'm putting a team of jackboys together, and I want you to lead them."

Maino focused his charcoal eyes on me, adjusted the Cuban link around his neck with the letters *PT* hanging from it, and stood up.

"You're wasting your time. The only team I run with is Pretty Tony. Now I got a dance to finish." He tried to walk away, but Menace and Wolf stood in his way.

"He's not done talking to you," Menace said with his arms folded across his chest.

Maino's face darkened. "Little boy, unless you're tired of breathing, it would be wise of you to move."

"I was born to die!" Menace shot back.

"Maino, this move would be beneficial to all parties involved. I'm Face, by the way. Listen, I can make it where you can rob and not worry about going to jail. You'll have jackboy immunity."

"You can't guarantee that type of shit," Maino turned back my way.

"I can but only if you're a part of Jackboy Mafia and you can still be Pretty Tony."

"Okay, I'm listening." He came and sat back down.

"This is how it will work. I'm trying to monopolize the jackboy trade. I want to get all the jackboys in the city under one umbrella first, then migrate to all the jackboys in the state. And eventually, I want to branch out to all fifty states with you leading them all. Everybody will get rich, and nobody will go to jail." I laid my plan out.

"All this sounds good but it's unrealistic. Better yet, it's impossible. You'll never get all the jackboys to agree."

"I said it wrong. I want all the heavy-hitting jackboys, fuck the small timers. And those that don't agree will be exterminated. It's gonna be get down or get laid down."

Maino leaned back, contemplating the plan I had laid out to him. On purpose, I didn't mention that I had the police on the payroll. It was a detail he didn't need to know at the moment.

"I'm with it," Maino said.

"There's one other thing though. You have to audition. I heard about you, but I want to see you in action."

"Say less. Let me know when."

"Probably tonight. Don't leave the club. I'll be back. Hold this." I handed him a Glock 40.

I got up and made my way towards the owner's office in the back, with Wolf behind me. Menace stayed with Maino.

"You're not allowed back here," a beefy bouncer said, and put his hand on my chest, stopping me.

I looked down at his hand and back up at him. I knew he was only doing his job, but tonight should've been the night he called in.

Wolf came around me, grabbed the bouncer's hand, pulled a hawkbill knife and sliced him open from his stomach all the way up to his chest. The bouncer fell to the floor with his intestines in his hands. Wolf was turning into a real asset. Wolf's white ass was all the way with the shits!

Wolf reminded me of the rapper Machine Gun Kelly. They were both slim, tatted and super lit. Wolf just had plaits that hung down his back, and had a mouth full of gold.

When we got to the office door, we could hear moans of passion coming from the other side of the door. We entered the office, and saw that the owner was fucking one of the strippers. He was in his chair behind the desk with his back to us, but she was riding him; so she was facing us. Her eyes nearly popped out of her head when she opened them and saw us standing there.

"Ahh!" She tried to cover herself up.

Warren, the club owner, turned around, saw us and started scrambling to get himself together.

"Nah, don't stop on account of us. Enjoy yourself. That might be the last nut you get." I leaned up against the wall.

"How the hell did you get back here? Tommy!" Warren yelled.

Warren had gotten his clothes on, and was standing behind his desk with the dancer behind him.

"If Tommy is the bouncer you had posted up outside, he had a bowel problem. So he's out of commission. Warren, I have a proposition for you and it would be wise of you to accept." I flicked a piece of lint off my YSL shirt.

"You need to leave my office right now! Warren was a bald head, light-skinned nigga with a beer belly.

"Warren, I need for you to sign the *Pearl Necklace* over to me. I'll make sure you're financially compensated." I ignored his yelling.

"Nigga, get the hell out of my club!" He picked his phone up.

I threw my hands up in surrender. "You got it. But remember you made your bed, now you have to lay in it."

Me and Wolf walked out of his office as shots started to ring out in the club.

Chapter Eleven

Boom! Boom! Kah! "Tali! Tali! TNT Gang!" The TNT gang was doing what they loved to do.

The entire time I was in the strip club, I had Soldier on the phone listening to everything unfold. If Warren agreed, they were to stand down; but if he didn't, then they were to rush the club. Contrary to Ox's belief, I had convinced the gang to use guns. Hearing his gang's chant, Wolf took off to join in on the festivities. I stepped over the dead bouncer in the hallway, and walked out onto the main floor. It was pure pandemonium! Everyone was scrambling, trying to get to safety, but there was really nowhere to go because the TNT gang was cutting up! I spotted Maino leaning up against the wall at ease, taking everything in. I got his attention and waved him over.

"This your doing?" he questioned.

"Yea. You ready to put some work in? We're about to rob the club."

"Say less."

We walked back into Warren's office. He was huddled in the corner with the stripper, talking into his phone.

"Hang that shit up, you sorry excuse for a man!" I shook my head.

Maino went and snatched the phone out of Warren's hand and slapped him with the Glock. He was taking charge.

"Where the safe?" Maino put the gun to Warren's head.

"I don't have one here!"

Boc! Maino shot him in the leg.

"Shit!" Warren fell to the floor, holding his leg.

"Oh my God! Oh my God!" the girl screamed.

Boc! Boc! Maino put her brain all over the wall.

Maino had passed the test already. Maino was going to be just what I needed to turn my vision into a reality.

"The next shot is going to end you, so what it's gon' be?" Maino aimed the gun at Warren's head.

"Behind the couch! 40, 23, 41, 36!" Warren yelled before passing out.

We moved the couch and saw the safe. I put the combo in, and it clicked open. Bingo! Warren obviously hadn't deposited his nightly take into the bank in a while because the safe was full.

"I can get used to this," Maino said.

"We need to hurry up before the jokes get here."

I took the bag out of the trashcan, and we loaded it up with money from the safe, but it wasn't big enough to hold all the money. Maino took off the red Givenchy shirt he had on, and wrapped the rest of the money inside. It was past time to go. *Boc! Boc!* Maino dome-checked Warren, and we took off. There were bodies littering the club floor from the TNT gang's rampage. They were posted up outside, waiting on me to come out. Upon seeing me, they all got in their cars and left, with the exception of Wolf.

"What are you driving?" I asked Maino.

"That red Range Rover sport," he pointed.

"A'ight, follow me."

Me and Wolf got in my Porsche and pulled out with Maino following us. I was going to go to *Pleasure's* to count the money up.

With Warren dead, the *Pearl Necklace* would be shut down. That's when I was going to swoop in and buy the building and open another strip club. Not only was I going to monopolize all the jackboys, but all the strip clubs as well. Then I was going to move on to regular clubs. In the next five years I was going to be extremely wealthy, and my team was going to be rich also. I wasn't going to get to the top of the wall and jump over. I was going to sit there and pull as many people as I could to the top with me.

We got to *Pleasure's* and pulled around to the back. Me, Wolf, and Maino entered through the backdoor, and walked to my office.

"The owner ain't gon' trip?" Maino questioned, sitting his money-filled shirt on the mahogany desk.

"I am the owner," I informed him.

"So that mean I can get some free dances?" Wolf said.

"That's below my pay grade." I tore the trash bag open and dumped the money on the desk.

We had just started counting the money when Pocahontas walked in, looking sexy as hell in a brown Fendi bodysuit that complimented her pecan-colored skin.

'What the hell?" she said.

"Don't *what the hell*, help us count this shit!" I told her.

"And risk breaking a nail," she dismissed me with a wave of her hand "Why don't y'all just use the money counters?"

Pocahontas pulled two money counters out and showed us how to use them.

They made life easier. Pocahontas sat behind the desk while we tallied the money up. The whole time, she was sneaking peeks at Wolf. My young boy was gon' get some of Pocahontas if his game was tight. The money came up to $375,000. I gave Wolf $30,000 to split with Menace, and Maino got $170,000. That left $175,000. I was going to give the rest of TNT $3500 apiece. I had to keep everybody happy. The $7,000 that was left over—I was going to send to Ox.

"Maino, you're the face of the Jackboy Mafia. You know the game plan. I'm putting it on you to recruit all the jackboys. Let me know of the ones who don't fall in line so their mama can go get fitted for a black dress."

"Say less. I'm out, bro." He dapped me and Wolf up and left.

"I'm about to blow some of this money on a stripper," Wolf said, standing up.

"Yea—me!" Pocahontas said.

"What are we waiting on?" Wolf openly admired her curves.

She led Wolf out of the office, leaving me to my thoughts. Everything was coming together perfectly! I had TNT putting it down. Maino was about to help me build Jackboy Mafia up. When word got out about what went down at the *Pearl Necklace*, the rest of the strip club owners should fall in line. I still needed to get Ox out of jail and kill Rude Boy.

"Yea?" I answered the unknown number.

"You thought you had the upper hand," Rude Boy responded. "You fucked up by bonding me out and sending those weak ass shots my way. Eye for an eye, you killed my brother and I killed your twin." He hung up.

Before I could call Trip, my mom called me.

"What's up, ma?"

"Trip's been shot!" she shrieked.

Chapter Twelve

I rushed out the club and hopped in the Porsche. My mom told me Trip was in surgery, and they weren't sure if he was going to make it or not. I was going over in my brain how Trip had allowed himself to be put in this situation. But then again, he had completely left the streets alone. He was completely invested in his football career, so there wasn't a reason for him to be on the alert. There was an added weight on my shoulders because had I not tried to be slick and bond Rude Boy out, this probably wouldn't have happened. I was feeling like I was the reason my twin was fucked up right now. God forbid if he died, I don't know what I would do. I was going to see to it that Rude Boy died before the week was out. I texted his picture to the entire TNT with the caption that I had $500,000 for his head. Rude Boy officially had my undivided attention—something he didn't want. I was about to touch him in every way possible. He was going to think I was the devil himself.

I was pushing the Porsche to the limit! I was doing 120 mph on I-95, trying to hurry up and get to Chapel Hill. My phone had been blowing up non-stop. Everyone was giving me their well wishes as if my twin was already dead. It was all over Facebook that Trip had gotten shot and was in critical condition

"Yo," I answered Murphs's call.

"Give Trip my love and me and Sha Loc on the way to Rude Boy's baby mama's house right now!" Murph's voice came through the car's speakers.

"Don't kill 'em—wait until I get back," I said and ended the call.

I wasn't in the mood, and I didn't have the right mindset to be talking to anyone. I kept replaying Rude Boy's comment in my head about how I had fucked up by bonding him out. If Trip died, it was going to be my fault.

I pulled into the hospital parking lot and rushed inside. I called my mom, and she gave me directions to where she was. I walked into the waiting area as a doctor approached her.

"Ms. Lowe, your son was very fortunate, him being in shape I believe is the only reason he made it—"

"So he's going to live?" My mom cut him off.

The doctor nodded. "We were able to extract all the bullets and repair the damage. The only problem is, he won't be able to continue his football career. One of the bullets damaged the tendons and nerves in his arm so bad that he'll never be able to accurately throw a football again."

"As long as he's alive I don't care," my mom stated.

I slumped down into one of the chairs. To Trip this was going to be the equivalent of dying. Since falling back from the streets and heading off to college, Trip's entire life revolved around football.

"Have you told him about his arm yet?" I inquired.

"He's heavily sedated right now and I felt like it would be best if he heard it from family."

I nodded, thinking the same thing, but I wasn't going to be the bearer of bad news. I was going to let my mom handle that. I could breathe better knowing that my twin was going to live. Now it was time for some get back.

"Where are you going?" My mom saw me getting ready to leave.

"Trip will live, so I can come back later but right now I gotta get this monkey off my back. And revenge is the only way to get it off."

"Kill all of 'em," my mom said, walking off down the hallway to see Trip.

Mama's approval was the next best thing other than God's. I knew God wasn't going to approve of what I was about to do, but we would discuss it when we met.

"We don't have anything to do with what you and Rude have going on," Rude Boy's baby mama pleaded.

We had her and their daughter tied up in the basement of the split level. Her name was Tiann, and their daughter's name was Tina. She looked to be about sixteen. I didn't care if she was two. Her daddy was Rude Boy, so she was about to pay for the sins of her father. When I got back to the city, Murph and Sha Loc had them tied up in chairs facing each other. I had zero sympathy for them. Rude Boy's bitch ass didn't have sympathy for my twin. I was sitting in the corner of the basement, watching the two. Murph and Sha Loc were watching me watch Tiann and Tina. I was having mixed feelings about the unfolding situation.

"What is it, cuz?" Sha Loc asked. "You act like you don't know what to do. Make these bitches suffer! Rude Boy got Trip laid up. Make him feel what you feel!"

I looked at my nigga, and I could see he was itching to get active, so I nodded at the hoes and said: "Do you."

Sha Loc smiled and left the basement. He came back down the steps with a duffel bag.

"Here we go," Murph shook his head.

I continued to sit there, watching.

"Please let us go!" Tina cried.

"I'll set Rude up for you—at least allow us to leave," Tiann begged.

I ignored them, watching as Sha Loc pulled a metal rod out with a metal ball attached to it with spikes on it. It looked like something from the medieval times.

"You gotta record this," Sha Loc said, and pulled a hood over his face.

Murph pulled his iPhone out and started recording.

Sha Loc walked over to the broads and swung the rod, sending the metal ball with the spikes into Tiann's face, splitting the left side of her face to the bone.

"Oh my God!" her daughter shrieked.

Sha Loc swung the rod again, connecting with Tiann's head, the rod getting stuck. He yanked it out, sending blood and a piece of her scalp onto my Amiri jeans, earning him a glare from me.

"My bad, cuz!" Sha Loc apologized, swinging the rod again, crushing Tiann's windpipe.

I looked at my nigga's face and saw a look of pure bliss.

I knew Sha Loc was crazy, but seeing him in action cemented the fact that he was all the way shot out. He continued to beat her with the rod and ball until her face was no longer recognizable. Rude Boy's daughter was silently crying, knowing that she was next.

"Now that's how you inflict some pain!" Sha Loc bragged.

"Man, she was dead after the first swing," I said.

"Don't sweat. That was only the preshow." Sha Loc dug in his bag, and brought out a container with what appeared to be fire ants.

I looked at Murph. Now I saw why he had been shaking his head. I had no idea what my nigga was about to do.

Sha Loc disappeared up the steps, and reemerged with some maple syrup.

Rude Boy's daughter obviously knew what was coming because she started trying to wiggle free.

"Please! Please!" she sobbed.

"Bitch, shut the fuck up! Your pussy ass daddy killed my girl and cut my unborn daughter out her stomach and hung her from the shower rail by her umbilical cord. You better be glad it's him and not me!" I snapped.

Sha Loc and Murph stared at me slack-jawed. They knew Rude Boy had killed Cynthia, but they were unaware of the particulars.

Sha Loc cut away her clothes until she was naked as the day she came into the world. He lost no time in rubbing the syrup all over her body.

"This shit better be good," I commented, ready to take over.

Sha Loc opened the container and sprinkled the fire ants all over her body. Immediately, the ants started biting her.

"Most people don't know it but fire ants originated in South America, and their bites contain little bits of poison. If enough of them bite you, it debilitates you, ending in death if not treated!" Sha Loc gave us a lesson.

"Aahh!" she screamed at the top of her lungs which gave the ants another spot to invade.

Tina's body was visibly swelling up. I nodded. I was impressed. After about fifteen minutes, she went completely still. Sha Loc then went in his torture bag, and came out with a blow torch. He proceeded to torch both bodies until they were burnt to a crisp.

"Send that video to Rude Boy's Facebook page and say *an eye for an eye*." I walked out; the smell had me nauseous.

I left the house, still in my feelings. I wasn't going to be satisfied until Rude Boy was dead, and I knew just the person to call for some help.

Nicholas Lock

Chapter Thirteen

I didn't have Detective Corrigan's phone number anymore, but I knew where I could find him—the police department. I was parked across the street, waiting to see Corrigan's suburban. I was going to get him to set Rude Boy up for me.

Corrigan's truck pulled out of the precinct and headed downtown. I pulled up alongside of him and blew my horn, getting his attention. I motioned for him to pull over. We pulled into a Circle K gas station.

"Sorry to hear about your brother," he said when I got in his truck.

The entire world knew about Trip getting shot; it was all over the news and ESPN.

"That's one of the reasons why I need to holler at you. I need you to set the dude up that shot him. I'll do all the dirty work. I just need you to get me his location."

"Who?"

"Rude Boy."

"That's easy. What else did you need to holler at me about?"

"I need more folders. A lot of them. I got some shit going on, and remember—the more D-boys we hit, the more money you make."

He looked at me as if contemplating giving me a folder, then asked: "Do you think you're ready for the big leagues?"

"I been in the big leagues," I said assuredly.

Corrigan raised his brow and grinned, showing me that now he had four gold teeth instead of the two he had when we had first met. They covered his four canine teeth.

"You're in the minors, but I'm about to bring you up to the major league. But I need you to realize there's no turning back, this will be a lifelong pact."

Hell! I was thugging with no brokes anyway.

"You ain't said shit!"

"Put this over your head and hand me your phone," he pulled a black hood out.

"I'm not putting that shit on!" I protested.

"Look, you're not allowed to know the location we're going to, and that trick you pulled with your phone to find out where you thought I lived isn't going to work this time." He let me know that I thought I was five moves ahead when really I was ten moves behind.

I gave him my phone, and watched as he took the battery out and tossed it on the backseat. I was going to play his little game for the time being. His secretiveness piqued my curiosity. He cut on some Marvin Gaye, as I put the hood on. We rode for about thirty minutes before we came to a stop.

"Leave the hood on—if you take it off before you're told, you'll die where you stand!" he threatened me for the second time.

"I've had enough of your threats."

Corrigan got out of the truck and opened my door. He helped me down and started leading me to the unknown location. We didn't walk far before I heard a door open.

"Jerry, you've lost your mind. Who the hell is he?" a familiar voice asked.

I knew the voice, but I couldn't put a face to it.

Corrigan replied: "Courtney, let me handle this. When you see who it is, I guarantee you won't have the same thoughts."

"It's his funeral either way," Courtney said. "Whether he walks out of here or gets carried out, it's not gonna affect me either way," she added.

Her last statement made the hairs on the back of my neck stand up. I had been biting my tongue, but the comment about being carried out killed all of that.

"Y'all got me fucked up!" I snatched the hood off and drew down.

When I took the hood off, I was face to face with Cynthia's mom! I hadn't seen her since Cynthia and our daughter's funeral.

"Nymel?" she gasped.

"Mrs. Weeks? What the hell is going on?" I lowered the gun.

She rushed up to me and hugged me. "It's so good seeing you again," she smiled.

Then her smile vanished and she said, "I don't know what Jerry told you but what and who you see here stays here. The circle of people downstairs are connected beyond your wildest dreams. You were me and Billy's only child's boyfriend and were going to give us a grandchild until Cynthia's life was stolen, so we love you. But we only have a certain amount of sway in the group. For you to be accepted, it takes for more than half of the members to vote *yes*. If you don't succeed in securing more than half of the votes, *you won't leave here alive*." Her voice turned somber as she laid emphasis on *you won't leave here alive*. "But I have faith in you, now come on."

I noticed we were at their house. As she led me and Corrigan through the house, I was as nervous as a whore in the front pew of the church. I wasn't nervous for the reason most would think. I was nervous because she told me I might not leave alive, and they didn't try to take my gun. We walked down into the basement, which was decked out. It looked like a high end bar and lounge. As we walked further in, I saw a large round table with ten people sitting around it, five of whom I knew. There was Cynthia's dad—Judge Weeks, my lawyer—Ms. Whitlock; the chief of police, who was white and tall with brown hair and a permanent scowl. There was also the sheriff, who was white as well, but heavy-set and short with black cropped hair. And the damn mayor of Fayetteville. He was a balding black man with a slim build, and stood about 6'0. They stopped talking when I walked into the room. Mrs. Weeks went and sat by her husband—Judge Weeks—and Corrigan took a seat, leaving me to stand alone. No one uttered a word. They all just continued to watch me.

"What up? I didn't come here to be stared at." I was starting to get anxious.

"Why did you come here?" a familiar, thick Hispanic chick asked.

"The better question is, who brought you here to die?" my bitter lawyer asked.

"I'm glad you said that because I can guarantee you this. Before I die, you'll die first and whoever else I can take with me." I pulled the .357 Glock back out.

Mr. and Mrs. Weeks smiled at my comment. Not one person flinched as I drew down.

"I like him," said a gorgeous Japanese woman sporting jet-black hair with red streaks. Her petite, 5'2 frame was perfectly proportioned. Her pert boobs sat up perfectly in her pink blouse. From where I stood it looked like she had a tootie booty.

"I'm the one who brought him here," Corrigan finally spoke up. "He's who I use to take care of the dope boys who refuse to pay. I feel he can be very beneficial to us and you would be doing a disservice to us all by killing him."

"Look here. The very next person who says a word about harming me will be swallowing a bullet!" I vowed.

"You talk a good game, but are those threats genuine or are they empty promises?" someone said from the shadows behind me.

I spun around and saw a white dude standing off to the side. I couldn't make out his features because of where he was standing.

"All you have to do is mention a word about doing me bodily harm, and you'll know first-hand!" I threatened.

If they thought I was going to bow down because the odds weren't in my favor, they had another thing coming. And what they had coming usually came with death.

He ignored my threat and said, "I heard from Jerry but I want to hear from you the benefit of us accepting you to the Elites."

"The Elites?"

"That's what our group is called. This is only a small fraction of our group. We have Elitists in every city and state across the states. Our reach doesn't end there. We have Elitists in different countries as well."

"And what exactly do you do?" I was somewhat intrigued.

"Whatever the fuck we want!" the group said in unison.

"Most of our members are in the legal profession, but we have members in other professions as well like Courtney, for instance. She's the only surgeon here. You already know Billy whom is a Judge. Detective Corrigan. And your lawyer, Ms. Whitlock. Then, you have the Chief of Police—Mark, Sheriff Thomas, Mayor Curtis, D.E.A agent Donovan, F.B.I agent Liu, State prosecutor Consuela, Federal prosecutor Matthew, Judge Jonas and me. We control the legal system. If we want you in prison, there's not a thing you can do about it, innocent or not. Now again I ask, what's the benefit of us accepting you?"

I know the Hispanic lady looked familiar. She was the D.A., and the Japanese woman was an F.B.I agent. D.E.A agent Donovan was the classic blond hair, blue-eyed white boy with an athletic build. Federal prosecutor Matthew was a young looking white dude with a head full of brown hair. He had some cold eyes. He was the man I had seen in Tasha's office the day I barged in. Judge Jonas looked prehistoric. He had to be about seventy years old, with a head of hair that had turned all the way gray. He was black with a fleshy build and an easy smile.

I didn't have an answer to the mystery man's question.

What the hell could I offer them that they didn't already have access to?

"What do you offer a man that has everything?" I questioned. "I'm trying to get to where y'all are. Right now I'm just a street dude trying to get rich and make sure my team is rich. It's not really what I can do for you as much as it's what you can do for me."

"Now that's some honesty for your ass. Son, if you would have said *anything* else, you wouldn't have been accepted. Welcome to the Elites. The *only* way out is through death." The mystery man paused, giving me a serious look before going on:

"You were wondering what you could offer us, and that would be your guns and your street smarts. You can give us an outlook from a street perspective, and all the while we'll be grooming you to the corporate suede of things. We have to make this thing official. By a show of hands, who's for him joining our group?"

Everyone raised their hands except Tasha, my lawyer. I knew what her problem was, though. I walked out of the Victorian house with full immunity. Streets, beware! It wasn't until I had got out of Corrigan's suburban that I realized the mystery man never told me who he was.

Chapter Fourteen

Before Corrigan let me out of his truck, he handed me two folders and said: "One of these is from Donovan. He heads the D.E.A on the east coast, so every folder that comes from him is going to have big payoffs but they're also going to have big risks." I nodded and got out.

I was opening my car door when a green Ford Explorer sped up to my car and stopped, causing me to draw my gun. The Explorer's door opened, and Laci stormed in my direction like a raging bull. I had been meaning to get at her, but she just wasn't high on my list of priorities.

"You ain't shit, nigga! I risked my job and freedom for you, and you couldn't call me not once!" Her voice was laced with pain.

"Laci, don't take it personal. You know the life I live. I be moving a thousand miles per hour. Hell, I'm still moving like a chicken with its head cut off. Where the fuck my hug at?"

She narrowed her eyes and reluctantly walked into my arms.

"Stop playing like you ain't wanna hug me." I grinned, hugging her short ass.

Laci was older than me by two years. We attended high school together, but didn't run in the same circle. She had given Murph Kameesha's address after Kameesha's brother—Ghost—had caught me lacking and put me in a coma. She'd also given me the address to one of my licks. I had fucked her after that. Laci was 5'5 and 200 pounds. She was pretty to the core. Although she was heavy-set, she wasn't sloppy. I fucked with her, and she had some of the best pussy I'd ever had in my life!

"You coming to my house?" she asked, and I read between the lines.

I couldn't deny her because she genuinely had my back.

"Yea, let's go."

I followed her to her apartment in Grove View Terrace. I knew she wanted some dick, and I felt obligated to give it to her.

Just like the last time I came to her spot, the same four girls were outside shooting Cee-lo again. They had so much money on the ground that I had to stop.

"Y'all gon' let me get in?" I questioned.

"Your money not long enough, playa," a redbone said.

"Huh? My money and my dick long." I pulled out a knot of money.

"Your money might be because I see your whip game is up to par," a chocolate chick said, eyeing the Porsche. "But I don't know about your dick."

"Oh bitch, it's long and good!" Laci chimed in, letting her presence be known.

"Let me find out, Laci," a brown-skinned chick with green eyes said.

"Nah, he's just my homeboy—for now." She pulled me towards her apartment.

"Damn, Laci, I was trying to win that bread."

"Boy, you not hurting for no money. I'm hurting for this dick though."

As soon as we got in her apartment, she started tearing at my clothes.

She got my clothes off and sunk to her knees, putting my soft dick into her mouth. The minute my dick felt the warmth of her mouth, it sprung to attention.

"Damn, Laci!" I palmed her head, leaning back against the door as she deep-throated me.

Laci was a man eater! She didn't have a gag reflex! Laci was taking my dick to the back of her throat and holding me there; she was even humming and massaging my balls. I was on the verge of climaxing.

"Suck this dick, Laci!" I said, gritting my teeth. "And you better not spit out." I was about to nut.

Laci didn't respond. She kept sucking my dick like she was auditioning for a spot in a porno flick. I held the back of her head, as I climaxed in her mouth. Laci swallowed my kids like they were a twenty piece combo from McDonalds. My dick was still hard as I sat down on the couch.

Laci peeled off the Gucci leggings she had on, and sat down on my wood.

"Fuck!" she said, rocking her hips to a beat in her head that only she could hear.

Laci's sugar walls were gripping me so tight I thought I was going to nut asap. I had to hold her still on my lap while I regrouped.

"This tight, wet pussy too much for your young ass!" Laci tooted her own horn.

"Got me fucked up!" I threw her legs over my shoulders and sank balls deep inside her love box.

I pinned her thick legs behind her head and put my stroke game down.

"Face! Face!" she yelled, as I pumped into her love box.

"Nah, this is what you wanted!" I said to her, as she tried to run from the dick.

"Here I come, Face!" Laci screamed as her legs started to shake, and she squirted all over my dick.

"Put this dick in your mouth." I pulled out and moved up until she was eye level with my manhood.

Laci opened her mouth, and ran her tongue around the head. I grabbed a handful of her sew-in, and fed her my wood inch by inch. I held Laci's head, and began to stroke her mouth.

She was taking my wood down her throat with no problem! I felt myself getting ready to bust, so I pulled out and started to jack off. I sprayed a handful of my kids all over Laci's face. I lay back, spent, watching Laci rub my cum all over her face and lick her fingers.

"You so nasty," I grinned.

"Only for your sexy ass," Laci said over her shoulder, as she went to the bathroom to clean up.

I needed to get up and go, but I was tired as hell. Just like the last time me and Laci had fucked, she wore me out.

"You want something to eat, baby?" Laci walked back into the room.

Baby? Oh lord, I was going to have to nip that shit in the bud before she got the wrong idea.

"Laci, don't be starting no crazy shit. We only fucking, so don't catch no feelings."

"Nigga, I'm a thug. I ain't got no feelings. You the one that needs to be worried about catching feelings, especially the way your face be looking when you be inside this box." She rocked her hips.

"Fuck you!" I threw a pillow at her.

I couldn't front, Laci was cool as fuck. If I wasn't so invested in Rai'chell, I'd give her big ass some play.

We smoked a blunt and kicked it awhile. It felt good to be able to let my guard down a little bit, but I knew it was only temporary. I left Laci's house and headed home. I had to spend some quality time with the wifey and my son because it was about to get hectic, and my free time was going to be nil.

Chapter Fifteen

"What the hell am I going to do now? Football was my life!" my twin—Trip—complained.

We were at our mom's house, and Trip was whining about not being able to play football anymore. I more than felt his pain, but I was going to leave the pacifying to my mom.

"Bro, what's done is done, all you can do now is move forward. Suck that shit up and man up."

"Man up? Nigga, I'll punch you in your mother fucking mouth!" he snapped.

"Aye, Trip. You only have one arm at the moment, so if you punch me, I'm telling you right now I'm gon' fuck you up!" I warned him.

"And I'm gon' shoot the shit out of you." He pulled a Taurus .380 out of the couch.

"Bro, you better stop playing with me! I understand you down and everything, but life goes on! Sulking ain't gon' change shit, nigga! A fuck nigga killed my girl and cut my daughter out her stomach! After a day or two, I was good. I couldn't let that shit continue to eat me, or it would've consumed me."

Even though me and Trip were identical twins, our demeanors were totally different. Don't get me wrong. Trip could get just as ruthless as me, but it took a lot to bring it out. Whereas—with me—something as simple as a look could set me off.

"That's because you evil ass don't give a fuck about nobody but yourself!" he yelled.

"I know y'all better stop all that yelling in my damn house!" my momma yelled, coming into the living room. "And stop arguing."

"Nah, ma, let him get it off his chest. I wanna hear this." I leaned against the entertainment center.

"You act like the shit you do is for everybody else, but in all actuality it's for your selfish ass. It's your fucking fault that I can't play football!" Tears were brimming in his eyes. "All you had to do was, accept that scholarship and come to UNC and play football! We both would be getting ready to play in the NFL."

"Selfish? Nigga, I didn't even know Rude Boy! But he shot Ross, and that's our nigga. So it was only right that I joined in to try and kill that nigga. Every fucking thing I do is beneficial to those around me! I bust down *everything* I hit for! Yet you say I'm selfish! You got me fucked up! Nigga, take that gun and put it in your mouth and swallow the clip!" I stormed out the house.

I was the most unselfish nigga on earth. I hopped in my Charger and peeled out. I couldn't believe Trip.

"Yea, man!" I answered my phone.

"Damn, nigga! I ain't did shit to you!" Rai'chell snapped. "Do you want me to go get the rest of your stuff from you and Murph's house?"

I was moving in with Rai'chell and my son until we found us a house that we liked.

"Nah, I'll do it."

"You been saying that for weeks, and it ain't got done yet! If you don't want us to live together, then say it!"

I hung up on her. I wasn't in the mood for her shit. She knew I was fully invested in me and her future.

"Yea?" I answered my phone.

"You remember who you asked me about?" Corrigan asked. "Well, it's a gray Lumina in the KFC parking lot on Owen Drive. He's in the trunk." He hung up after giving me the info.

I texted Murph and told him to meet me at the KFC on Owen Drive.

This was going to make my day. I was about to take out all my stress on Rude Boy's hoe ass.

When I pulled into the KFC, Murph was already there. Luckily for us, he had Ross and Sha Loc with him. I got out the Charger, and walked straight over to the Lumina. The keys were in the ignition. I popped the trunk as my niggas walked over to the car. They still didn't know what was going on.

"Oh shit!" Murph said, seeing Rude Boy bound and gagged inside the trunk.

I slammed the trunk close.

"Ross drives this and follows me. Murph you drive behind him."

I was about to fuck Rude Boy's world completely up! I pulled out with Ross behind me, and Murph and Sha Loc behind him.

I didn't wasn't to risk Ross getting pulled over. We got to the house across the river, then Murph and Ross carried a struggling Rude Boy into the basement.

"Let me get 'em, cuz—I got some new shit from Tyrone, and this is the perfect time to use them," Sha Loc said.

"A'ight, but he has to suffer, and I mean in a nasty, gruesome way too."

"Done." Sha Loc got in Murph's new Bentley Bentayga, and swerved off.

I chuckled because when Murph realized his truck was gone, he was going to blank out his mind.

I walked in the house and down into the basement, and they already had Rude Boy tied to a chair.

"Where Sha Loc?" Murph asked.

I started laughing. "He took your truck to go get something." Murph shot out the house.

"Mr. Rude Boy, it's been a long time coming but I got you now and we're about to have some fun." I circled him.

Pow! Pow! Ross two-pieced him. "That's for shooting me, fuck nigga, but the best has yet to come."

"Why you let him take my shit!" Murph barged back into the basement, mad as hell.

"Man, bra! He coming back." I snatched the gag out of Rude Boy's mouth.

"Let me go and I'll take you to four million dollars," he pleaded

"Where is it?" The jackboy in me peaked its head out.

"Y'all come help me real quick!" Sha Loc yelled.

We all went outside where Sha Loc had the Bentayga up to the front door with the back open. I looked inside and saw a huge fish tank filled halfway up with water, with piranha inside. The piranha weren't moving, though; they were just floating in the water like they were dead.

"I wouldn't dare put my hands nowhere near that tank." I walked back in the house.

A few minutes later, Sha Loc, Murph and Ross came down the steps, gingerly carrying the fish tank and sat it in front of Rude Boy. Rude Boy looked down into the tank and said: "The money is in a safe in a trailer at the end of Deep Creek Road, the combination is 1, 2, 3, 4, 0."

Sha Loc grabbed one of Rude Boy's legs and sat his foot in the tank. The instant his foot touched the water, the piranha snapped to life. They attacked Rude Boy's foot with a vengeance.

"Stop! Stop!" Rude Boy struggled against the ropes.

Sha Loc lifted Rude Boy's foot out the water, and there was nothing left but the bone.

"Oh shit!" Ross said.

"Hold him!" Sha Loc yelled, grabbing the blow torch he'd had from the last torture session, and torched the nub. "We don't need him bleeding out."

"Rrrr!" Rude Boy groaned.

"Don't you holler now, nigga! You weren't hollering when you killed Cynthia and my daughter." I felt myself getting mad.

"I didn't kill them!" He yelled, gritting his teeth.

"Nigga, I saw your car leaving! You're going to die in this basement regardless, so you lying helps you none."

"I loved Cynthia. When I got there, a girl was rushing out of Cynthia's apartment. I went in and found her already dead. That's when I ran out and swerved off." He dropped his head to his chest, on the verge of passing out.

"Man, let me continue!" Sha Loc was ready to torture him some more.

"Hold up. So a bitch killed Cynthia and cut her stomach open and hung my baby from a shower rail?" I smirked. "I'll give it to you. You're gonna ride that lie until you die. Humor me, what did she look like?"

Rude Boy lifted his head, looked behind me and said: "Her."

Boom! Boom!

Two slugs slapped Rude Boy's chest, and he clumped over into the fish tank still tied to the chair. I turned and saw Rai'chell holding a smoking gun.

Nicholas Lock

Chapter Sixteen

"What the fuck, Chell! I wasn't done with that nigga!" I looked down at the tank where Rude Boy was halfway devoured.

"That nigga is the reason Trip is fucked up," she defended her actions.

"And where the fuck you get that hammer?" I looked at her.

"Better yet, where you learn to shoot like that?" I inquired.

"Watching you, baby, and I told you a lot has changed. I'm not that same naive girl from school."

This was the second time she'd told me that. I looked at my niggas, and they all had a crazy look on their face.

"Chell, that's the second time you done told me that. Is it something you wanna tell me?"

"Yea, I love you," she smiled.

I really knew Rai'chell—deeply. I think I knew her better than she knew herself. So I knew when she wasn't being truthful.

"Chell, this nigga said you're the one who killed Cynthia, why he say that?"

"I don't know! I didn't know that bitch ass nigga." She tried to keep a straight face, but there was something beneath the expression.

Again I looked at my niggas, and this time they were shaking their heads. They were getting the same vibe that I was.

I turned back to Rai'chell, and her smile was gone, replaced with a menacing sneer.

"I told you if you ever played me, I was gon' fuck your world up, you remember?" Chell asked, walking down into the basement.

"Yo, y'all niggas need to leave. Me and my husband need to talk." They all looked at me.

Boom! Boom! She let off two shots. "Why are y'all looking at him? I said I need to holler at my husband in private." Rai'chell had transformed. She had a look on her face similar to the one I wore when I got on my bullshit.

"Face, what's up?" Ross asked.

Before I could respond, Rai'chell said: "Oh, you niggas got me fucked up! Y'all don't think my gun blow or something? Tell you what. In five seconds, if y'all are still down here in this basement, I'm gon' let this .40 talk!" She had adopted all my mannerisms. Somehow, the shit was low-key sexy.

"Let me holler at her real quick," I said before shit got out of hand. She put me in a bad situation because my niggas was hardened street niggas, so they weren't scared of the gun she was wielding.

They reluctantly walked up the steps.

"Mean mugging ain't never killed nobody, but it's gotten a lot of niggas killed!" Chell told Ross.

"Chell, bring your ass here!" I yelled. "Now what was it you about to say?" I asked when she came over to me.

"You played me, Nymel, after I warned your ass." I know she wasn't about to say what I thought she was.

"You say that to say what though?" I squinted.

"I followed Cynthia to her apartment so I could talk to her. She knew who I was. Obviously, you had told her about me. She let me in, and I told her she needed to leave you alone because you were still mine even though we were taking a break. Then she told me that wasn't possible because y'all were about to get engaged, and she threw it in my face that she was about to have your baby and I snapped."

I found this confession shocking. I took a deep breath, as my mind replayed the scene I walked into with Cynthia laying dead in the bed with her stomach sliced open and my baby hanging from the shower rail.

"Rai'chell Marie—" I called her by her first and middle name. "Tell me you didn't kill Cynthia and my daughter."

I didn't get a response at first, then she said: "It's your fault. You shouldn't have got her pregnant in the first place." I had never put my hands on Chell, but I found myself itching to fuck her up. I was torn because I wanted to hurt her, but at the same time she was also my son's mother and my first love. Rai'chell could tell too because she moved out of my reach. What the hell was I suppose' to do? Could I kill her and cause my son to grow up without a mother? Had this been anybody else, they would be face down in the tank with the piranha. The more I looked at Chell, the more I felt myself beginning to hate her. I walked out the house, got in my Charger and drove away. I needed to clear my head. I turned the radio on, and one of me and Trip's favorite song was playing—"Live in the Sky" by T.I.

I had to call my twin and apologize.

"What's up, momma?" I answered her call.

"Trip killed himself!" she screamed.

Chapter Seventeen

"Life's ups and downs, they come and go / But when I die hope, I live in the sky / All my folks who ain't alive, I hope they live in the sky / Pray to God when I die that I live in the sky / It's true what goes around comes back, you know / So when I die, I hope I live in the sky / All my folk who ain't survive, may they live in the sky / Tell God I wanna fly, and let me live in the sky." The chorus to T.I.'s 'Live in the Sky' was playing at Trip's funeral.

I was sitting on the front row. My mom was beside me, crying her eyes out. I turned around and saw all my niggas. I even saw motherfuckers I hadn't seen in a minute. Then my eyes landed on Rai'chell and my son. We hadn't talked since her revelation about killing Cynthia and my daughter. I was mentally exhausted! I got the news about Rai'chell's treachery, then five minutes later I got word that my twin killed himself. And that was after I told him to swallow the clip in his gun. I was so numb I wasn't even able to shed any tears. I was too young to be dealing with this kind of shit. But they said what didn't kill you made you stronger. Angie must have sensed my mood because she reached over and grabbed my hand.

"It's gonna be okay," she whispered.

I was back staying with her again. I couldn't bring myself to go to Chell's. Angie welcomed me with open arms. I could always count on Angie to have my back regardless of the situation. If she wasn't so caught up on her being twenty-four years older than me, we'd be in a relationship. Angie never nagged me. She kept me fed, and she felt like it was her mission in life to keep my dick satiated. The only time she denied me pussy was when her period was on, and then she made up for it with her mouth and ass.

The funeral was a blur. I was there just physically. Mentally, I was a million miles away. Really, I was lost. Usually, I would be planning my revenge mission but who was to blame? Was I suppose' to kill myself being that I told Trip to kill himself and he did it? I didn't ride in the limo to the burial site; instead, I drove the Porsche. I had '*Live in the Sky*' on repeat. Trip was being buried in the same cemetery as Cynthia and my daughter. When we got to Rockfish Memorial, I walked to Cynthia and my daughter's grave site. This was my first time visiting their graves. They were side by side. I placed a bouquet of carnations on each of their graves, and took a seat between the two.

"It's been a while, Angel. You probably thought I had forgot about you, but know that's not the case. My love for you is as strong as it was when you were here. I have to give it to you. You were right about the club thing. *Pleasure's Paradise* is doing numbers! I could stop all my nefarious activities right now and just rack up the money from the club, but you know that's not in my pedigree. Your girl Pocahontas is running the club, and she makes my life so easy. The only time I go to the club is to pick up the money. Also, I'm about to lock down the entire club scene in Fayetteville. You may not like how I'm doing it but—baby, I'm confused. The whole while, I thought Rude Boy was the one who had killed you but it was Rai'chell. Am I suppose' to kill her? Then where does that leave me and her son? Damn, I need to talk to you, to hear your voice. And I know you and I know you probably would say: *Let it go and live life*. Regardless of my decision now, I love you, Cynthia. You'll always be my Angel. I leaned down and kissed her pink marble headstone.

I turned to my daughter's grave and said: "Princess, you were stolen from me before we had a chance to meet but I know you're up there with mommy, so you're good. I want you to know daddy loves you. I wish I could hold you, baby, and it kills me to know that I never will. You went to the place where all the good people go, and your daddy hasn't been very good. You be good for mommy. Remember your daddy loves you to the moon and back." I kissed her headstone and stood up.

I went back to Trip's funeral, and went through the motions. At the conclusion, I saw Diqueena; I hadn't seen her in a while. I went over to her, wrapped her up in a bear hug and swung her around.

"Oh my God! Face! Put me down. I ain't got no panties on, boy!" she shrieked.

"Where the hell you been, girl?"

Diqueena was one of my best friends. She was also Rai'chell's best friend. We used to kick it all the time. Lately, we hadn't been seeing each other as much as we used to. I checked out her 5'0 frame; her dark skin was still as pretty as ever, and her Jhene Aiko-like body was perfect for her little frame. Her thick, silky black hair had grown, and was now about three inches below her shoulders. Her high cheeks and thick lashes complemented her perfectly structured face. In short, my homegirl had turned into a full-fledged baddie.

"Stop looking at me like that, boy!" Diqueena's dark chocolate ass turned shy.

"Like what?" I faked ignorance.

"You know what, boy" She punched me in the arm. "Anyway, how you been?"

"You know me. I just been going with the flow." I shrugged, looking as the funeral broke up.

"Face, when have you ever just went with the flow? Nigga, you are the flow! My momma said you better stop being a stranger too."

"I got you. Here go my new number, call me so I can take you shopping." I took off because I saw Chell making her way towards us, and I wasn't ready to deal with her yet.

I hugged and kissed my momma, letting her know that I was about to go.

"Don't blame yourself, Nymel, you know he loved you. Here—" she handed me an envelope with my name on it in Trip's handwriting.

"Love you, ma." I walked off, and sat down in my Porsche.

I opened the letter and it read:

Nymel,

Bro, you know it's all love and it's no hard feelings. We're identical twins. So physically, we're just alike but mentally and emotionally, we're opposites. Where you're outgoing and have an extrovert personality, I'm naturally an introvert. Bro, without football, my life has no purpose. My decision has nothing whatsoever to do with our argument, we've been arguing for eighteen years. Just make sure you take care of momma and continue to give these fuck niggas hell! I love you, bro, and I'll be waiting on you in hell because I know we gon' take that bitch over. Then again, knowing you, you'll probably get us kicked out of hell. Lol!

P.S. Jack or Die!

I was laughing and crying at the same time. Trip had lifted a huge weight off my chest. I had no choice but to honor my twin's wishes. I was gonna jack or die trying!

Chapter Eighteen

I looked at one of the folders that Corrigan had gave me and saw a nigga I had went to school with. His name was Luda. People called him that because he looked like Ludacris. Luda was the pill man. If what the folder said was true, and they hadn't led me wrong yet, then Luda was doing a'ight. It said he had at least half a million at his spot, and if you caught him on the day he went to re-up, you would come off with at least 300,000 pills. They were a variety of pain pills from Percocet's to Xanax's. I opened the folder from Donovan, and didn't recognize the Mexican man in the picture.

"Bingo!" I yelled to no one in particular.

I was going to hit this one personally. His name was Diablo, and he had that work. He was part of the Sinaloa Cartel, the cartel headed by El Chapo. The folder stated that Diablo was one of the largest distributors of black tar in the southeast. Black tar was said to be the strongest heroin on the market. The folder said Diablo was playing with at least 300 bricks. That many bricks of uncut boy would put Ross ahead of the game for a while. I could only imagine what Diablo's cash was looking like. And Rude Boy hadn't been lying about the four million dollars. We went and checked the trailer. Really and truly, that money was in the safe. Me, Ross, Sha Loc and Murph all got a million apiece. Sha Loc went crazy, seeing all that bread. Me and Murph had been sitting on over a mill, so it wasn't nothing new to us. I invested my million in TNT. I gave all fifty of them twenty thousand. They all went crazy. They had never had that much money before. To me that was a small price to pay. They were going to be the reason that I got ten times that million. Then Maino had recruited three jackboys—whom I approved of—to the Jackboy Mafia. First, there was Snub—a short, stocky, brown-skinned dude with shoulder-length dreads. He was from the Westside. Rico—a short, light-skinned dude with long hair—was from Lafayette Plantation. I fucked with Rico, and I went to school with his older brother—Chub. Then there was Streets, a dark-skinned, slim, super active nigga from the Murk. I called Maino and told him to meet me at Super King buffet on McPherson Church Road. I looked in the closet, and pulled out a dark green sweatsuit with some matching green and black low top Air Force 1's. I grabbed an emerald green Baltimore Orioles fitted with the black brim, and sat it on the bed. I got dressed, put on a few dabs of *I Am King*, and left Angie's house. Moneybagg Yo's new single—"Got Time"—bumped out the speakers as I cruised through the city. Chell had been blowing my phone up, but I wasn't ready to deal with her yet. I needed some more time. I called Murph, and he answered on the first ring.

"What up?" he asked, sounding sleep.

"Get your ass up! I got us one. It's a big fish too."

"A'ight, give me a minute."

"Meet me at the Sonic on Hope Mills Road like twenty minutes, and bring two vests and that new Carbon 15." I ended the call, then called Wolf.

"What up, big bro?" he answered.

"You trying to get active? And what's all that noise in the background?"

"Pocahontas got her homegirls over here and they acting stupid."

"Meet me at the Sonic on Hope Mills Road in twenty minutes," I said and hung up.

Since they had met, Wolf and Pocahontas had been inseparable. Every time I called Wolf, Pocahontas' ass was somewhere in the vicinity. She had latched onto my young boy and wasn't letting him go. I had took a liking to Wolf's crazy ass too. He was all the way with the shits, and didn't give no fucks. And his drip game was something akin to mine. Me and Maino pulled into Super King's parking lot at the same time. He came and got into my Charger.

"Here, bra." I handed him the folder.

Maino flipped it open and nodded. "I'm gon' round the niggas up, and we gon' handle this asap."

"Do your thing," I said and dapped him up.

Maino got out, and I took off towards Sonic. Fifteen minutes later, I was pulling into Sonic's where I saw Wolf and Murph rapping with two white girls.

"Whenever y'all ready," I pulled up on them. I waited while they got the snow bunnies' numbers and came and got in.

"Check it out." I tossed the folder in Murph's lap.

He read over it, looked at me and smirked, then handed the folder to Wolf.

"It's this where we're going?" Wolf asked excitedly after reading the folder.

I nodded and smiled. I pulled the vest over my head, and checked the clips to the Carbon 15.

"Put that on." I tossed the other bullet-proof vest in the backseat to Wolf.

I didn't need to get him a gun, because he had a Draco. The folder said Diablo had took over Golden Gate trailer park on Fisher Road. Golden Gate was another one-way-in-and-one-way-out spot, which I hated. But luck would have it that the trailer that all the work was supposed to be in was in the back. This made it where we wouldn't have to go through the front because the neighborhood Aaron Lakes was right behind Golden Gate. So, all we would have to do was: park in Aaron Lakes and hop the privacy fence that separated the two, and we'd be right at the trailer.

"I got an idea," Wolf offered.

"What up?" Murph asked, reading back over the folder.

"I can get some of TNT to give us a diversion at the front of the trailer park and while everyone is at the front, we'll have little resistance in the back."

"I like that, make it happen," I said.

Wolf was showing me that not only was he about blowing smoke, but he could also think—a trait that would keep you alive and out of the legal system. While Wolf set his plan up, I drove to the back of Aaron Lakes and parked. There were people out raking their yards, which was going to make our job that much harder. The last thing we needed was a good Samaritan calling the police. We were just going to have to deal with it as it came because there was no way I was letting this lick pass me by.

For all the good luck I'd been having, I knew it was about time for some bad luck. That bad luck came as I looked in my rearview mirror, and saw two cop cars pull up behind me and cut their lights on.

Chapter Nineteen

"Driver, cut the car off and throw the keys out of the window!" one of the police officers said over their loudspeaker. Murph and Wolf looked at me to see what I was going to do. They were way more worried than me. I knew that no matter what, we were to the good. I was just mad at the timing of the situation. Being an Elite, I knew I had immunity.

Boom! Boom! Boc! Boc! Kah! Kah! You could hear the gunfire in Golden Gate trailer park from where we were. A call must've come over their radio from dispatch because the two cops that were harassing us pulled off.

"Let's go! Let's go!" I said, getting out the car.

We ran and hopped the privacy fence, scaring the white people who were out doing their yard work. I wasn't worried about them calling the police. Even if they did, they were going to be more worried about the gunfight going on than three people hopping a fence. We ran straight up to the trailer, and Murph kicked the door open. I was the first one through the door. Instead of me seeing bricks of boy, all I saw was an empty trailer.

"What the fuck!" I yelled after going through the whole trailer.

"This might be the wrong one," Wolf said.

"Even so, we don't have enough time to go trailer to trailer," Murph said.

I wasn't trying to leave empty-handed, but what else could I do?

I looked out the blinds to make sure the coast was clear, and saw some Mexicans loading bags into the bed of a blue Dodge Ram 1500 at the trailer behind us.

"Come here!" I said, pointing at the window for them to look.

"Let's go!" Wolf was eager to put in some work.

"Wait. How about we let them load all the bags in, then we just take the truck?" Murph said.

"I'm with that right—But they're having a whole live shoot out at the only entrance into the trailer park," I said, still hearing shots towards the front.

"Why don't we just go back the way we came?" Wolf asked, like it was no big deal.

"Maybe you forgot but there isn't a road that way. You do know we had to hop a privacy fence to get here." Murph's voice betrayed his frustration.

"Make a road," Wolf said, causing Murph to snort in disbelief.

I think I understood what Wolf was trying to say.

"Put me behind the wheel and I'll show you what to do," Wolf said smugly.

"Say no more." I saw that the Mexicans had pulled the cover over the bed of the truck.

I came out the back door, firing the Carbon 15. *Tat! Tat! Tat!* I hit two of the Mexicans, dropping them. Wolf and Murph dropped the other four, leaving us in the clear. I wanted so badly to check the trailer that they had been taking the bags from, but the shots towards the front had all but stopped. So I knew our time was up.

"What are you waiting on?" I asked Wolf as I got in the passenger seat of the Ram.

Murph got in the backseat as Wolf got in the driver seat. The keys were already in the ignition. Wolf took off like he was driving to the entrance, then hit a U-turn.

"What are you doing?" Murph asked, obviously unaware of what the plan was.

I put my seatbelt on as Wolf floored the Ram, causing the Hemi under the hood to whine. The closer we got to the privacy fence, the more Murph yelled.

"No! No! Let me out! Let me out!"

We hit the privacy fence at close to 70 mph. The big boy pick-up truck smashed right through the fence with no problem. The people that were out just stared at us slack-jawed. Wolf stopped by my car to let me out.

"Meet me at *Pleasure's Paradise*." I got in my Charger, and swerved off in the direction of the club.

Meanwhile Across Town—

"Check it, this should be a quick in and out, we gon' take this nigga for all he got and some. No slip-ups." Maino gave this instruction to Snub, Rico and Streets.

Rico had stolen the black Durango that they were riding in. They were on their way to Savoy Heights, where Luda had a crib with his girl and their three-year-old son.

"Damn, bitch, slow down!" Streets fast-talking ass told Rico.

"I got this," Rico grinned, turning Kodak Black's new mixtape up.

Maino turned the music down, as they approached Luda's house.

"How we gon' get in the house?" Snub asked.

"Thug style," Streets said, smirking.

Rico pulled into Luda's driveway, and they got out. Streets took off running towards the front door, and kicked it off the hinges, never breaking stride. You would've thought he was incapable of that feat, because he was skinny as hell at 6'1 and weighed 165 pounds. Maino, Snub and Rico were right behind him. They caught Luda as he was scrambling out of the bed, reaching for a pistol.

"Too slow," Streets said, kicking Luda back onto the bed with his girl.

Luda's girl was so scared she couldn't even scream.

"It's only one way this is going to go and that's with you giving us the pills and money," Maino said.

"And please save all the I-ain't-got-nothing talk," Snub chimed in.

"What you gon' do, man? I got shit to do!" Rico was getting aggravated.

"Mommy!" Their three year old son ran into the room and hopped up onto the bed.

"Bra, I ain't got shit!" Luda said.

Boc! Boc! Streets put two .45 slugs in the little boy's chest.

"Aahhh—" *Boc! Boc!*

Luda's girl's scream was cut short by the two .45 slugs that entered her mouth courtesy of Street's Springfield.

"The next ones are for you so what it's gon' be?" Snub said.

Luda looked at this dead girl and son, then back at Streets. You could feel the hate radiating out of his body. The look he was giving Streets could only be interpreted one way. Obviously, Streets knew it too because he said, "This is what you get for being stubborn and uncooperative!" *Boc! Boc! Boc!* The slugs from the Springfield blew the bottom portion of Luda's jaw across the room. Maino could only shake his head.

"Let's find the work so we can go," Maino said.

They found the pills in the refrigerator in Ziploc bags. Then they found Luda's money, which was in the bottom of the living room couch. There were exactly 500,000 pills. The money came up to $730,000. Face had told Maino how to divide the money up so all of them got $131,000, and the

$206,000 that was left over was Face's but $73,000 of it went to Corrigan. Maino dropped the money off to Face at *Pleasure's Paradise* before going home, while Rico went home to his girl. Snub and Streets stayed in the club to trick.

***

Me, Wolf and Murph pulled the cover off the truck behind *Pleasure's* to see what was in the bags.

"*Hoooly* shit!" Murph said, opening one of the bags.

"This looks like a foreign car to me," Wolf said.

Every bag we opened was filled with money. I wondered where all the work was. My only guess was that when the shooting started, they loaded the bricks up and got low—which was why the trailer was empty. We probably had gotten lucky by catching them before they could get low with the money. We took the bags inside, and let the money counters do their job. When it was all said and done, we tallied up seven mil. We all got two mil apiece, and Donovan got $700,000. We agreed to put the $300,000 that was left over to the side for shit like guns. Besides, we were about to throw a party and it would cover the expenses.

Chapter Twenty

"I'm sorry to call everybody here on such short notice, but we have a situation that needs addressing," Billy said.

All the Elites were meeting again. Everyone was there, except the white dude that did all the talking last time. I assumed Billy was the de facto leader.

"It seems as if Allan has decided he wants to blow the whistle on our group, and that's something we can't allow," he said.

"Who is Allan?" I asked.

Billy continued: "He wasn't here the last time we met, so you didn't meet him but he's a member. He wants to be the leader of the Elites, but the position is already taken and now he says that if he isn't made the leader then he's going to the press."

"Another question—Who is the leader? I'm asking because no one told me," I said.

"The man that you threatened," Tasha reminded me.

"You mean to tell me you didn't recognize him?" Mayor Curtis said.

I shook my head. "No," I replied.

Billy got my attention almost immediately. "Back to the matter at hand. We cannot allow Allan to go to the press about the Elites. He has to be silenced!" Billy banged his fist on the table.

"Why don't we send the new boy to silence him?" Tasha flashed a sarcastic grin.

Me and Tasha was going to have to get a level of understanding because she was starting to get on my nerves with her snide remarks.

"I don't know about that," Consuela protested, and Tasha snorted in disbelief.

"I ain't met a motherfucker yet I couldn't handle," I said with plenty of confidence.

"Sounds like he's volunteered, so let him do it!" Tasha urged.

"Face," Chief of police—Mark—called my name, making me pause.

I don't think I would ever get used to being cordial with the police. It's like it was embedded in my DNA to be leery of them.

"We've been onto you. Your name has been a hot topic since you started robbing, so we're more than aware of your capabilities *but* Allan is head and shoulders above you. While you shoot a hundred rounds, hoping to hit something, Allan can shoot ten rounds and kill fifteen people."

"You act like he's Special Forces or something," I said.

"Delta Force, to be exact!" Tasha smiled.

My mom always told me my mouth would get me in some shit one day, and I think that day was today.

Delta Force was top of the food chain in the military world, them and the Navy Seals. The government called in Delta Force for high risk missions, and they didn't fail.

"Give me his address and info and I'm gon' take care of him," I said.

Billy slid a piece of paper down the table with everything on it I needed to know.

"Don't let us down," Courtney looked me in the eyes.

"I don't plan on it," I said and walked out.

Tasha was about to push the button to start her Bentley when I grabbed her by the ponytail the instant I hurled myself in through the backdoor.

I whispered in her ear: "I don't know what your mother-fucking issue is, but I'm starting to feel like you're coming for my neck. And that's a real good way for you to lose your life."

"Let my hair go before I yell," she said.

"And I'ma paint the windshield red!" I warned her.

I let her go, and she turned towards me with fire in her eyes.

"Don't you ever put your hands on me again or I'll cut your fucking throat!" Tasha threatened me.

"Save your idle threats, I don't care for them. We need to get some kind of understanding. So what's your issue?"

"You! It's niggas like you that make us look bad. I did my research on you, and you had scholarships from every division one school in the nation to play football. And you graduated with a 4.0 G.P.A. but instead, you want to frolic around in the streets. You have the potential to be anything you want to be but you'd rather be a common thug!"

"Bitch, you don't fucking know me because if you did, you would know that I'm a successful business owner. Every single person around me is straight! While you see a thug, I see a nigga that's helping motherfuckers live a life they wouldn't be able to live otherwise, so what if it's illegal! And let me ask your holier-than-thou ass something. Without crim-inals where the fuck would the world be?"

"In a good state," she said quickly.

I chuckled. "You think so? So if nobody broke the law, why would you need criminal lawyers, judges, police, jails and prisons? The only motherfucker that deserves to be in prison or death row is the sick individual who rapes women and kids." This statement of mine left her speechless. "Cat got your tongue? Make sure you get Ox out of that box asap." I opened the backdoor to get out.

"I might not be able to," she said, making me pause.

"Huh? I thought we controlled the legal system and could do what the fuck we wanted?"

"We do."

"I hear a but coming."

"The cop that he killed was an Elite."

Chapter Twenty-One

Tasha had dropped a bomb on me last night with her revelation about Ox killing an Elite. That was going to be a very delicate situation. I wasn't a hundred percent sure; but, reading between the lines, it was sounding like Ox was going to have to do some time. I was going to try and prevent it, but the hole he had dug himself in might be too deep for me to help him out.

I had just left Diqueena's house where she had snapped on my head. She had put the fish bones in my hair, and they were all the way like that. In the short time I had been allowing my hair to grow, my hand time was already a little past my shoulders. I was dressed head to toe in black. I was on war time. I had to take care of this Allan guy. I wasn't going alone, though. I had a little more sense than that. I was on the way to meet Murph, Wolf, and twenty members of TNT. With Allan being in Delta Force, I knew we were going to have our hands full. I was going to try and overwhelm him. I had gotten some intel from my nigga— Tyrone—about Allan. With Tyrone being in the military, he had more insight to the way Allan moved. He advised me to leave the man alone unless I was ready to reunite with Trip. Once he saw I was dead set on going, he strapped me all the way up. He gave me a P90 assault rifle with armor-piercing bullets. An AK-74, a Kalashnikov, a rocket launcher and some night vision goggles—all of which he said I would probably need. I could understand the dude was a Delta Force pro and all, but people were making it seem like he was Superman or Incredible Hulk. Allan was still flesh and blood. I met up with everybody at the shopping center at the corner of Yadkin and Cliffdale Road.

"I need y'all best right now because the person we're about to go kill is trained for this type of shit. *We* have no room for error. TNT, y'all are going to be a red herring more than anything."

"What's a red herring?" one of them asked.

"A distraction. Now look, all y'all have to do is get this dude gunning for y'all while me, Murph and Wolf creep through the back."

"That's easy," Menace said.

I passed out the guns I had gotten from Tyrone, but I kept the night vision goggles and the rocket launcher. I didn't want them blowing nothing up. We got in our cars and left. Allan stayed on the outskirts of Fayetteville on the Hoke County line—in a five-bedroom single story house. Me, Murph, and Wolf parked at the woodline by Allan's house, and got out while everyone else went to the front.

"Let's get to it—Pocahontas is cooking tacos tonight," Wolf said, checking the Tec. 9.

I put a round in the chamber of my M4 while Murph checked the H&K MP10 he had slung across his chest. We walked through the woods until we could see Allan's house. He had the only house you could see. The houses in the neighborhood were so spaced out that we weren't going to have to worry about any outside interference. There was something nagging at me. It was like the shit was too easy. I saw the cars pull up in front of the house, and TNT got out. Allan must've been looking out the window and sensed that they weren't there to sell him some candy, because he started shooting. I saw one of the TNT members fall to the ground, then all hell broke loose. The rest of them started shooting at the house. Delta Force or not, he was forced to take cover. We took off towards the back of the house. Murph hit the backdoor in full stride, knocking it all the way off the hinges. Obviously, Allan wasn't expecting this because he tried to take off down the hallway, and Wolf's Tec mowed him down.

"That was easy as hell," Murph said, walking over to a crawling Allan, and used his foot to flip him over.

"You fucked up, homie," Wolf said to Allan.

Bllt! Bllt! I ended his career with a burst from the M4. There was a sword hanging from the living room wall, giving me an idea. The Elites thought very highly of Allan, so I was going to taint his image and bring them his head.

"I know you not about to do what I think you are," Murph said as I grabbed the sword off the wall.

"Yes, he is," Wolf grinned, as I brought the sword down on Allan's neck, severing it from his body.

I looked around and spotted a bowling bag. I dumped the ball out, and put Allan's head in it.

"You done lost your damn mind." Murph shook his head.

"Savage life! Fuck it." Wolf loved that turn up shit.

The TNT members rushed to the front door, and Wolf let them in.

"Niko got hit in the arm but he's good," Menace said, walking in the house.

"He's lucky it was only his arm," I said, looking at all the awards on the wall for marksmanship. "Tear this shit up. Whatever you want you can have."

"Oh shit! Who cut his head off?" Tonya gasped.

"Face," Wolf said.

"This is mine!" Ogun held up the sword I had used to cut off Allan's head.

"I'ma catch up to y'all later." I walked out the backdoor while sending a group text to the Elites, telling them that we needed to meet—it was urgent.

***

"What the hell was so urgent that you got us here at eleven o'clock at night?" Sheriff Thomas asked.

"Yea because I have trial tomorrow," Federal D.A. Matthew stated.

"As do I," Tasha cosigned.

"Maybe if y'all let him speak, he'll tell us!" Billy spoke up.

"Thank you." I got up from my seat and started walking around the round table. "I'll make this quick and to the point. Allan is a thing of the past. He was killed earlier tonight."

"I just can't believe that," F.B.I. agent Liu said in a disbelieving tone.

"I kinda figured that's how the news was going to be received so I brought you all a gift." I put the bowling bag ball on the table, and pushed it over so that Allan's head rolled onto the table.

"The fuck!" Chief of police Mark stood up from the table.

"Oh my God! What have you done?" Judge Jonas stared wide eyed at the head.

"What's the problem?" I was confused.

Tasha looked to the skies and sighed. "Face, you've succeeded in waking a sleeping giant."

"I'm outta here." Corrigan got up, looking spooked.

"I thought y'all wanted him dead."

"We do, Face, but that's not Allan—That's his youngest son," Billy said, and then all the lights went out.

"What the hell!" Donovan said.

"He's here," Corrigan whispered.

I put on the night vision goggles I had around my neck, and saw everybody groping around in the dark.

"Y'all need to sit back down," I said, pulling the Desert Eagle off my hip.

Everyone mumbled their dissent.

"Just do what the fuck I said!" I said harshly. "Or at least stop moving." They did as I said.

I knew that to get to us, Allan had to come down the steps. I started moving towards the bottom of the steps when the hairs on the back of my neck stood up. Something wasn't right. I was always taught to go with my first instinct. I turned back towards the room and saw a man aiming a gun my way. I was able to get off a shot, but not before he placed four shots dead in the center of my chest, knocking me on my back. The gunshots were deafening inside the walls of the basement. My chest felt like it was ripped open. The vest I had on had stopped the bullets, but it still felt like I had gotten shot. I knew I had to get up because I wasn't sure if I had hit him or not. When the shots rang out, everyone panicked and began to run in the blind. I rolled over onto my stomach as the lights flicked back on.

"Oh my God!" Consuela gasped somewhere to my right.

"Get up," Tasha grabbed my arms.

She helped me up, and that's when I saw what Consuela had seen to make her gasp. Allan was up against the wall in a sitting position with his head barely hanging on. The slug from the Desert Eagle had torn through his neck, almost severing it. I limped out the house and took my ass home. I was going to get Angie to give me a massage. I'd let them clean the mess up since I had done all the heavy lifting.

Nicholas Lock

Chapter Twenty-Two

Megan Thee Stallion's hit—"Don't Stop"—was bumping out of the speakers in the club as I sat in my office, contemplating my next move. My plan was steadily coming together. Not only had I secured the building, but I had secured *Diamonds and Pearls* as well. Next, I had my sights set on *Secrets*, which had a more upscale feel to it. I was going to turn *Secrets* into an exclusive gentleman's club. There was going to be a strict dress code, and you weren't going to be able to come inside without getting $7,000 in singles. That would eliminate the pretenders and wannabes. And I was going to have straight foreign bitches inside that knew how to get a sucker out of their bread. So I knew if you came in with $7,000, they were going to get you out of at least $3,000.

"What are you doing here?" Pocahontas asked, walking into my office.

"Damn, am I not allowed to come to my club?"

"Boy, boo. I'm just not used to seeing you here, that's all."

Her statement let me know that I needed to show my face more and maybe take a more hands-on approach in the every-day activities of the club.

"When are you gonna stop dancing?" I asked, looking at her with her titties out and a G-string on. "I know you're not hurting for no money."

"Big facts. Face, I've never had to strip. My brother spoils me to no end. That Maserati truck outside came from my brother, the condo downtown came from my brother. I strip because I like it. I like the power I have over a nigga as I look back at him and make this ass clap. The look of lust these nig-gas have when I grind this pussy on their hard dick. The sad-ness that be in their eyes when the dance is over and their pockets are a few racks lighter."

"Tricks is what I call them, but whatever floats their boat—" I shrugged.

"The world is full of tricks."

"I've learned that everybody has a role to play in life. From the junkies to the prostitutes, to the police. Junkies keep the D-boys with a job. Tricks keep the prostitutes with a job."

"Prostitutes?" Pocahontas scrunched her face up.

"Let me clarify something. I say *prostitute*, and a lot of y'all are prostitutes nowadays. Hold up." I saw she was about to snap. "Look at the lyrics to the songs that Cardi B, Nicki, Megan Thee Stallion and the City Girls be rapping. Don't get me wrong. I fuck with them. For instance, "Pussy Talk" by the City Girls. They say nothing but a bag makes that pussy talk. What's the difference between being a prostitute and a chick fucking a nigga for a Birkin bag and some red bottoms? I don't knock it, but you got to call a hoe a hoe. It don't matter if she a million dollar hoe, she still a hoe."

"So you wouldn't pay to fuck none of them?"

"Outright no. But yo, if JT say she needed the new Chanel clutch, she got me. I want her! But I feel like I could fuck them for free. I'm a hell of a nigga. A lot of people get that celebrity shit twisted. They're no different than you, they're just celebrities. That don't mean their pussy different."

Pocahontas busted out laughing. "Nigga, you different as hell but I fuck with you. You know you're the *only* nigga I ever danced for and didn't feel like I had any power over."

"I'm not a trick."

"I bet if I danced for you now I would," she walked over to me.

"Nah." I stood up and walked out the office.

She was my little nigga Wolf's bitch, and I wasn't about to go there. There were lines that real niggas wasn't suppose' to cross, and having your man's bitch dance naked for you was one of them—even if she was a stripper.

I walked into the dressing room, and all the strippers started giving me hugs and kisses. I sat down at one of the stations, and addressed them all.

"Are there any complaints, or is there anyway y'all feel the club could be better?"

"Yes! I want to be the headliner sometimes and I'm not the only one that deserves it," said a pretty, blond-haired, blue-eyed white chick with more curves than a country back road.

"Why do you feel like you deserve it?"

"This right here," she pulled two knots out that were probably ten racks. "And I made all this in four hours."

"But how much of that came from sucking dick?" Danielle's sexy ass asked.

"Bitch, fuck you!"

"Aye, y'all can kill all that right there because I ain't got no time nor the energy for it. So y'all can put aside whatever differences y'all have or there's the door."

"You need to tell that trailer park trash to stop whining and bitching all the time," a thick redbone said.

"I'm tired of it too," said a chocolate baby doll.

I saw what was going on. All the dancers that Pocahontas had brought with her or hired had formed an alliance against the other strippers. But I was about to crush their bubble.

"What's your name and you say you ain't had a chance to headline since you been working here?" I inquired.

"My name's Fire, and no—I haven't headlined since I began working here," she said with her arms folded.

"Next Friday, you're the headliner."

"Thank you!" She kissed me on the cheek and strutted away.

"That was suppose' to be my day!" Danielle pouted.

"Come on, ma, I know you done headlined at least fifteen times. Share the wealth, Brown Sugar." I used her stage name.

"Nigga, you owe me." She narrowed her eyes.

"How much I owe you?"

Danielle walked over to me and whispered in my ear: "This dick."

"Only if you bring a friend," I said, and walked out of the dressing room.

I walked out onto the main floor and took everything in. I saw the bottle girls in their black booty shorts with the pink P's on each cheek and their pink halter tops with black P's all over them, taking bottles everywhere. I saw the bartenders with full bars, serving drinks. Everything was to the good. I looked and saw all the VIP sections were booked, then I saw Ross in one of them.

"Nigga, what you got going on?' I walked in his section.

"Chilling, waiting on the plug to show up."

"Oh yea?"

"No, Face, you can't rob them." He read between the lines.

"Never crossed my mind." I sat down on the couch.

"Sure," he said in a disbelieving tone. "Here come the plug now."

I looked up to see who the plug was, and my jaw dropped. It was Lauren and her sister—Karla!

Chapter Twenty-Three

Lauren and Karla saw me sitting on the couch, and had two totally different reactions. Karla narrowed her eyes, but Lauren lit up.

"Hey, nigga! You ain't on no bullshit, are you?" Lauren asked.

"Nah, baby girl, it's all over," I reassured her.

"Wait a minute. Y'all know each other?" Ross asked.

"Yea, we know that bitch ass nigga!" Karla snapped.

Ross looked at me, knowing I was about to straighten her ass but Lauren beat me to it.

"Bitch, get your shit together and get out your feelings! You should be thanking that nigga because he prevented his homeboy from killing us."

See, the way me and Lauren and her sister met was under less than ideal circumstances. Lauren happened to be the girlfriend of a nigga me and Murph were robbing. His name was Karma. He and his brother—Lucky—came to Fayetteville from New Jersey, and had the heroin game on smash. I had robbed his brother about a week before. Me and Murph caught him lacking in his backyard in the pool with Lauren and Karla. In the process, Karma and Lauren got into it because she told us where his stash was. Then the shit went all to hell! Lauren's amazon ass got to fighting with Karma. He grabbed her by her neck and produced a .380, putting it to her head as if me and Murph gave two fucks about her. But when her little sister—Karla—jumped in, things went south for Karma. Then Murph gets the bright idea to tuck his gun and try and break them up. Karla grabbed Karma's nuts, allowing Lauren to get the gun. She proceeded to blow Karma's head off, and then put the gun on Murph's dumb, stupid ass! Somehow, I convinced her to give Murph the gun. That was the moment he slapped her to the ground and was about to kill her, but I stopped him. I saw something in her. Karma had a safe that required his hand to open it. I told her she needed to cut his hand off. I was testing her. She cut his hand down to the bone, and she snapped it off! She had that killer instinct! Me and Murph were up at the time, so I let them have the money in the safe and their lives. Obviously, they had took advantage of the situation.

"So how did y'all meet?" Ross inquired.

"Through one of my ex-boyfriends," Lauren quickly interjected, and cut her eyes at me.

She obviously didn't know me and Ross' relationship because I was going to tell him what was up. I looked at Lauren's amazon ass, and couldn't help but stare. Lauren was 5'11, 180 pounds with an even mocha complexion. Her double D's sat up high and perky in the black Balenciaga long-sleeved dress she had on. Her body was outrageous! The Balenciaga dress hugged her body like a glove, showcasing the fact that she didn't have a waist. Her ass was stupid big! I'm talking Cardi B, Nicki Minaj big. Then her chinky eyes and naturally long eyelashes gave her an exotic look.

"I'm gonna let y'all handle y'all business." I got up and walked out of the VIP section.

I walked to the bar and grabbed a seat.

"Let me get a double shot of Goose."

"Hey stranger," the bartender said.

It was the white girl with the burgundy and purple hair.

"Hey you," I said, downing my drink.

"Face, can I be honest with you?" she asked as she sat another drink in front of me.

"Of course." I downed the drink.

"I wanna suck your dick. I want you to nut all over my face and in my mouth."

"As much as I'd like to, that just wouldn't be professional," I told her and walked off before she could reply.

"I owe you," Lauren came up to me and hooked her arm into mine.

"For what?"

"For not allowing your homeboy to kill us and for letting us keep the money. You know Karma was using me to ferry his drugs from up north, so I was familiar with the real plug. I used the money from Karma's safe to get on and I haven't looked back."

"You don't owe me shit, Lauren, just get that money," I said and tried to walk away, but she grabbed my arm.

"Where are you going?" She moved closer to me.

"To mind my business."

"I'm coming with you," she thrust her DD's in my face.

"Lauren, I ain't fucking with you. You'll never kill me in my sleep." I pinched one of her nipples and strolled off.

***

"Bro, I'm trying to get you home but shit done got complicated. One of the cops that got killed was a somebody." I explained to Ox.

"I already know. That lawyer came to see me yesterday. She told me in so many words that I would probably have to go do a bid."

I had come to see Ox. I wanted to tell him straightforward it wasn't looking good. I felt like I owed it to him.

"Bro, I been preparing myself to do a bid since they locked me up. You got my account looking good, so I ain't got nothing to complain about. And you got my gang eating. I'm straight! The only thing I ain't getting is some pussy."

"I'm gon' see what I can do about that but other than that, what's been up?" I asked.

"Same shit, different toilet. Oh—and Ms. G. been asking about you too. She keep asking for your number. Shit, she working right now. Ms. G!" He called for her.

"Man, I ain't thinking about her ass," I said, then she walked onto the screen.

"Oh nigga, I'm about to go on break, wait for me," she said in the screen.

I just nodded.

"Nigga, what you smiling about? I only agreed because I'm trying to get you some pussy," I admitted.

"Good looking either way," he continued to grin.

The screen started flashing, letting us know that the visit was over.

"Hit me, bro, and stay sucker free." I hung up the phone and went outside.

Ms. G only had about five minutes before I took off. I sat on the hood of the Porsche, and rolled up a blunt. I had just got some Girl Scout cookies, and I was dying to see what it smoked like.

"You don't give a fuck! How you gon' sit out here and smoke some gas in front of the jailhouse?" Ms. G asked.

"When you got bond and lawyer money, you don't sweat going to jail," I smirked. "What you wanted me to wait for you for?" I looked her up and down.

Her slim-thick frame made the jail uniform look good. At thirty-seven she still looked like a girl half her age.

"Just because—" She looked me up and down.

I knew she liked what she saw. I was dripping like a fool! I had on a pair of black Dolce and Gabbana straight legs, a blue t-shirt with the words *Rich Forever* across the front, and some black and blue Foamposites. I had on my gold rosary, and I had just bought a Patek Philippe watch with diamonds all through the face and band. My braids were still fresh, but I had them covered with a black Dolce and Gabbana beanie. I nodded at the Porsche and we got in.

"Yo, my nigga Ox might not be getting out no time soon. I need you to help him relieve some stress for me."

"How I'm suppose' to do that?" Ms. G turned her body towards me.

"Give him a shot of pussy." I wasn't beating around the bush.

"You got the wrong one," she pouted her thick lips up.

I leaned my seat back and unzipped my jeans. I grabbed her by the back of the neck, and put her face in my lap with no resistance.

Ten minutes later, I filled her mouth with my kids.

"Now go in there and tighten my man up." I tossed a knot of money in her lap.

"I wanna sit on that dick too, nigga." She put the money in her pocket and got out.

I shook my head and pulled off. It was time to get back to work.

Nicholas Lock

Chapter Twenty-Four

"I don't know who it is—I know it's none of my people," I informed Corrigan.

Someone was robbing niggas and shooting them in the ass again. Whoever it is, they had stopped for a little minute but now they were starting back up. Corrigan was concerned because some of the dudes that were getting robbed were paying him.

"You need to find out who it is and do something about it." He handed me four more folders. Lately, Corrigan had been keeping the folders hot.

"I'ma see." I hopped out his truck and into Murph's red Ferrari Portofino.

"What it's looking like?" Murph asked.

I handed him one of the folders to look at. The one I had had to have come from Donovan because the face staring back at me was none other than Alvaro Calderon—a Colombian drug lord! I had seen him on the F.B.I.'s *most wanted* list. After El Chapo, who had been number one on the list, next came Alvaro. He was alleged to be Pablo Escobar's illegitimate son, which put him at the head of the Medellin Cartel, the biggest and most ruthless cartel in Colombia. I couldn't understand what he was doing in the States—and Fayetteville to be exact. Furthermore, why wasn't the government going after him? I was going to pick Donovan's brains on the matter the next time we met. I was happy that the government wasn't going after Alvaro because to hit Alvaro Calderon would be the sting that would make me hang my ski mask up. At least in the active side of things. I would still have the Jackboy Mafia doing their thing. I would just be focused on becoming the king of the nightlife. I had assessed my plan on owning all the strip clubs and nightclubs. Now I was just going to own all the high-end clubs; the hole-in-the-wall spots I could care less about.

Maino wasn't playing any games when it came to recruiting for Jackboy Mafia. He had added four more heavy hitters. If truth be told, as far as Fayetteville went, there weren't any more jackboys worthy of being under the JBM banner. There was Abdullah, a twenty-eight-year-old light-skinned, Muslim nigga with a brush cut. He was about 6'0, 185 pounds. He was from Baltimore, but he had moved to Fayetteville three years ago. I fucked with him the long way! He was also a chubby chaser, he loved big girls. Next was G'd Up—a 6'5, 245 pounds' dark-skinned dude from the outskirts of the city. G'd Up was a big country-bred, country-fed nigga. He had a penchant for violence. He was also twenty-eight. Next up was a young boy named Ratchet—a 6'4, 220-pound brown-skinned nigga with dreads. At sixteen, Ratchet was a vet in the rob-a-nigga gang. Then there was a dyke named Desire. She was eighteen and caramel-colored, and stood about 5'8. I wasn't able to see the type of body she had because she always had on nigga clothes. She was pretty, but her demeanor would let you know not to holler at her. She didn't do *meat*, period—and you could tell by her mannerisms. Desire acted more like a dude than some dudes I knew. Her robbery game was top-notch, though! I had heard of plenty niggas that had made the mistake of thinking shit was sweet when she had her fire on them, and they ended up wearing a shit bag or either losing their life.

"This is one for the crew—It's that nigga from the Westside named Fever that sell powder," Murph said, handing me the folder he was looking over. I picked up another folder and saw it was a girl named Lucy. She was a sexy redbone, with fire-red hair. It said she was a scammer; she popped checks and credit cards. The folder said she had at least $100,000 at her house.

I was going to tuck this one. Instead of hitting her, I might recruit her to my team. If she was really like that with the scam game, I could definitely use her. The last folder was a nigga from Ramsey Street by the name of Angel. He sold meth, and was one of the few people in the city that dealt with it. The folder didn't have how much money he was sitting on, but I knew it wasn't petty. I called Maino and told him I had two more folders for him.

"Two?" Murph looked at me quizzically.

"You know we gon' hit the Colombian, and I think I might can use the scammer bitch." I gave him my reason for only giving Maino two folders. "When did you get this Ferrari?"

"This ain't mine, it's the dealership's," Murph said.

Murph had took my advice and started the exotic car dealership. He had everything from Lambo's to Maybach's. I was going to get the Rolls Royce Wraith; it was my dream car. We drove to Maino's house, dropped the folders off and left.

"Look at your bitch," Murph pointed, and I looked and saw Rai'chell in the McDonalds parking lot on Skibo Road, talking to a group of girls. The closer we got, I recognized the girls. They were the same four chicks I always saw shooting Cee-lo when I went to Laci's. I was wondering how she even knew them.

"Bra, pull into the Burger King." The Burger King sat directly across from the McDonalds. I had to see what the hell she had going on. They were just in the parking lot, chilling, then a white Maserati Ghibli pulled in with two niggas inside.

"That's Fever right there," Murph referred to the nigga in the folder we had just gave Maino.

Fever and his homeboy got out, walked up to the girls, and started talking to them—with Fever in Rai'chell's face. My temperature shot to the moon when I saw Fever grab Rai'chell's ass and leave it there. Murph looked at me, seeing my reaction. As fast as I had gotten mad, I cooled off. Shit, I didn't own her. So if she wanted to fuck with another nigga, who was I to say something. He leaned down and whispered something into Rai'chell's ear, and she nodded. The next thing I knew: Fever and his homeboy got back in the Maserati, then Rai'chell and the girls got in a black Navigator.

"Follow them," I said, putting one in the head of my Glock .29. I was about to rob the shit out of Fever! We followed them to the Westside into Remington. They parked at a two-story brick house and went in. Murph already knew what time it was because he cocked his twin .45's. Murph parked four houses down, and we got out. The sun had just set, so it was dark, but the moon was casting enough light for us to see. We stood on the side of the house for five minutes, giving them enough time to relax and let their guard down.

Pop! Pop! Two gun shots went off inside the house. Me and Murph came around the house as Chell and the girls came running out the house, carrying bags and guns! Chell saw me and Murph, and her eyes got big. The other girls pointed their guns our way, and we did same.

"No, wait!" Chell stood between us. "They're good."

Then the nigga Fever limped in the doorway with an AK-47, but that proved to be the worst mistake of his life. We all turned to him and let off! It sounded like the fourth of July! Fever's body jerked like he was having a seizure as we filled him with bullets. The jokes were on the way, and I didn't plan on being there when they arrived.

"Follow us!" Chell yelled, getting into the Navigator.

Everything had happened so fast. As shit was starting to slow down, I realized that they had robbed Fever and shot him in the ass. They were the ones robbing niggas and shooting them in the ass.

Nicholas Lock

Chapter Twenty-Five

We followed Chell and the girls to the Holiday Inn Express. They already had a room booked. Me and Murph followed them into the room. Rai'chell tried to hug me, but I held her at bay.

"We ain't on that kind of time yet, nigga," I told her.

Me and Chell had yet to sit down and have a conversation.

"What the fuck you got going on? You robbing niggas and shit! And where the fuck my son at?"

"He's at Diqueena's," she huffed.

"This your baby daddy?" the thick, brown-skinned chick with green eyes asked.

"Yes, this is him," she placed her hand on my chest.

Me and the petite, pretty redbone made eye contact, and she raised her brow. I subtly shook my head, hoping she didn't tell about me and Laci.

"So y'all the ones that's been robbing and shooting niggas in the ass—which is dumb as fuck, might I add," Murph said.

"Anyway, nigga! We been doing hella good, probably better than you two niggas!" the super thick but average looking dark-skinned girl said.

"You think so?" Murph questioned. "I'll tell y'all what. If y'all count all the money from the lick and it's more than the money I got on me, I'll give each of you a Ferrari but if I got more, y'all got to give me the money."

I looked at Murph like he was crazy.

"Come on, let's count this money," an ugly yellowbone said.

I grabbed Chell as she tried to walk over to the bed where they had dumped the money.

"That robbing shit is dead! Make this your last time doing that dumb ass shit!" I snapped.

"Ain't like you give a fuck about me no more. I'm starting to think you and that old bitch Angie fucking!" She folded her arms across her ample chest.

"Don't try and flip this shit around on me, and I see that nigga palm your ass and you ain't do shit but smile."

"Somebody jealous," the redbone said.

"Bitch, you might want to mind your business!" I snapped.

"Really?" the brown-skinned girl asked, and I read between the lines.

She wasn't telling Rai'chell about me and Laci, so I had to tread lightly.

"I ain't say shit because I had to get the trick ass nigga to let his guard down. Face, you know this body is yours even though you don't want me anymore." She pouted. "And let me introduce y'all. The brown-skinned girl with the green eyes is Sidney, the redbone is Marquita, the dark-skinned girl is Tatianna, and the yellowbone is Jasmine. Y'all, that's Murph and this is my baby daddy—Face."

"Chell, you know I want you but—I just need some time," I confessed.

"I understand." She stood on tiptoes and kissed me on the lips. "Baby, these are my girls and I'm their leader. I wouldn't ask you to turn your back on Murph and them, so please don't ask me to."

"She's got a valid point," Murph said.

"Don't gas her up, nigga!" I warned.

"It's thirty-three thousand dollars, nigga!" Jasmine said to Murph.

Murph started laughing. "I got more than that in one pocket."

He pulled out his money and counted out $40,000, crushing their hopes and dreams of getting a Ferrari.

"You're not getting that money though," Rai'chell interjected.

"How did you know you had more money than us?" Sidney asked.

Murph smiled. "Because y'all weren't in the house long enough. I bet y'all only grabbed the money and work that they willingly gave you."

The girls nodded.

"Always remember that the big money is the money that the nigga is unwilling to give you. And all the big timers have a stash." Murph gave them the game.

"Why don't you take us on a lick and show us how to do it the right way?" Marquita asked.

Murph looked at me.

"Hell no, nigga!" I said.

"Bro, an all-female crew in JBM would be the icing on the cake," he tried his pitch.

"What's JBM?" Tatianna asked.

"Jackboy Mafia," he answered.

The more I thought about it, the more I could see Murph's vision.

"Please, daddy!" Chell looked up at me with those bedroom eyes.

"Y'all only get one shot!" I said, and walked out the room.

I was battling myself because I really wasn't feeling Chell robbing. Nevertheless, being that she would be with four other girls, the odds would always be in their favor.

"Never hesitate, always shoot first and ask questions last. Because there's no second chances if a nigga puts one in your head!" Murph coached.

"I'm about to take this vest off," Marquita said.

"That's on you but wearing a vest has saved my life a few times," I admitted.

We were in Jasmine's black Navigator on the way to Raleigh.

I had a lick lined up to see how they were going to act.

"You need to focus!" I yelled at Chell because she kept rubbing on my dick through my jeans.

"Boy, I'm good! You don't think I picked up on nothing from being around you? I can suck your dick, put a hollow point in a nigga's face then come home and play with Nymel."

My bitch was cold-blooded! Me and Chell had kinda, sorta made up, but I still wasn't staying with her.

We got to Raleigh, and I gave Marquita directions to the Southside to Martin Street. The dude we were about to hit was a nigga named Stew. He sold dog food; I had met him back when I was selling weed.

"Look now, Marquita. You better be able to whip this big motherfucker because we might have to high tail it out of here." I said so because Martin Street was the hood, and if niggas got wind of what was going on, they were going to get active.

"She's the best driver in the group," Tatianna said.

"Say no more. Park in front of that white house right there," I pointed.

It was 10:30 at night, and Stew's spot was jumping! We all got cut, and no one paid us any mind. That was a plus. No one expects a bitch to rob them. We walked right up to the open front door, and went in. The minute we crossed the threshold, me and Murph pulled out and put the hammers on Stew and the dude he had with him. All the junkies took off running, as the girls followed our lead. I looked back at Rai'chell, and she got the hint because she went into action.

"Who else is here?" She ran down on Stew, and he only looked at her.

Boom! She shot his homeboy in the face and turned back to Stew, putting the .40 to his lips.

"Who else is here and where is everything at?" she asked again.

Murph took Jasmine and Sidney to clear the rest of the house.

"The work is in the freezer and the money is in the trunk of the Honda Accord outside," Stew said through gritted teeth.

Marquita went outside to check the car while Tatianna checked the freezer.

"This how you do, Face?" Stew asked.

"Just business, homie." I shrugged.

Tatianna pulled two birds out of the freezer as Marquita came in carrying two red duffel bags.

"You a bitch ass nigga for this, Face!" Stew said.

Boom! Chell put the back of his head on the wall

"Let's go!" Chell yelled.

We were running to the truck when the door to the house next door opened, and niggas came mobbing out. *Boc! Boc! Boc!* They started shooting in our direction. Me and Murph turned their way and began to return fire, and so did the girls, causing the dudes to take cover.

"Start the truck!" I yelled to Marquita, and she took off.

We made it to the truck just in time because niggas started coming out of every house on the street! We made it off Martin Street, and were on the way back to Fayetteville when Wolf called me.

"What up, bro?" I answered.

"Bro! Menace, Tonya and three other TNT members got killed!" he yelled into the phone.

"What? By who?"

"That Mexican dude we robbed—Diablo!"

Chapter Twenty-Six

How the hell did Diablo know where to find Menace and them? Was he going to be satisfied with the blood he had drawn? Really it didn't matter because TNT wasn't going to let it go, they were about to go live!

The whole TNT was in the parking lot outside of *Pleasure's Paradise*, itching for some action.

"Who the fuck is this wetback?" Oshun asked.

"He's a somebody in the Sinaloa Cartel. His name is Diablo. He's not to be taken lightly. You know them cartel dudes are of a different caliber."

"I'm not to be taken lightly either and while they're of a different caliber, I don't have a caliber." Oshun's face darkened.

"We're done talking!" Ogun matched his sister's demeanor. "Tali! Tali! TNT! TNT!" he yelled, setting the rest of the gang off.

There was no talking to them. I could tell that just by their energy. I looked at Murph, and he shrugged like it was whatever. A yellow Camaro pulled up to us with a Mexican inside. I instantly drew down, and he smiled.

"For you," he tossed a flip phone out the window at my feet, and burnt out.

I picked the phone up and saw it had an active call.

"Yo," I said, putting it to my ear.

"Face, you took something that not belong to you and you need to bring it back," a voice said in broken English.

"Who is this?" I asked, but I had a good idea who it was.

"Diablo. Me watched as you took the truck full of money and left. I know you, you not know me."

"Get it in blood!" I threw the phone across the parking lot.

I knew we should have searched that trailer that they were bringing the money out of.

"That was Diablo, wasn't it?" Murph asked.

"Yea. Y'all ready to terrorize some shit?"

"Tali! Tali! Tali! TNT! TNT!" was their response

"Let's go." Me and Murph got in the Mustang he'd rented, leading the way to Golden Gate.

"Get it in Blood" by Poo Sheisty—featuring Lil Durk— was playing as we made our way to Golden Gate trailer park.

I was going over in my mind how the hell did Diablo know who I was and where to find me! That shit wasn't sitting right with me.

"Pull over," I told Murph.

"What up?" Murph asked, pulling into John Griffin Middle School.

"How did Diablo know who we were and where to find us?"

"That was kinda funny," he admitted.

"Why did we stop?" Ogun yelled out the window.

"Because something isn't right. He knows too much about us yet we know nothing about him," I said.

"So what!" one of the Tiaras yelled.

"I'm trying to save y'all. To go at Diablo blindly will end in a lot of death." I tried reasoning with them.

Hissing, Soldier said: "We're going with you or without you. He spilled TNT blood, now it's time to spill cartel blood."

"Y'all will listen to me next time," I warned.

We drove into Golden Gate and didn't see a soul. It looked almost deserted. We drove all the way around the trailer park, and were coming back to the entrance when two F-150's blocked the only way out. I looked behind us and saw Mexicans coming from everywhere, shooting assault rifles! I told those stupid motherfuckers! I came out the window with the choppa, spraying the F-150's out of our way because in our position we didn't have a chance at winning. There was just too many of them. They were coming in waves. *Boom!* One of the F-150's exploded, the explosion flipping it into the air on top of the other one, clearing the way for us to escape. We sped out of the trailer park like a bat out of hell. I looked behind us and noticed we didn't have the same amount of cars that we started with. We pulled over, and I got out. We were two cars short!

"It was nothing we could do," Wolf said. "There were too many of them."

I looked and saw that Oshun and Ogun were still alive. I breathed a sigh of relief.

"You see what the fuck I mean! I told you motherfuckers, but you didn't want to listen! Look at you now! Next time I tell you motherfuckers something, it would be in your best interest to listen!" I spazzed. "That wild, reckless mentality works sometimes, but you still have to use your head!"

"Fuck all that! I want my shot at being alpha!" Soldier got out one of the cars. "I'm more equipped to lead us."

"What! I'm making you niggas rich! You're not capable of that."

"Are you ducking this rec?" Soldier asked. "Either you're going to give me my shot or give me the reigns to TNT."

"You know what? You can have that shit, nigga, let me see what y'all bag look like a month from now. Let's go, Murph." I turned to walk away.

"Fuck! I thought I told y'all he was a bitch ass nigga!" Soldier said, stopping me in my tracks.

"I tried, bro," I said to Murph.

Murph shrugged and said, "Whoop his ass."

"This what you want? Come on then, little nigga!"

Soldier ran up to me and swung a haymaker that I ducked. I caught him on the chin with an uppercut that put him on the ground. Soldier scrambled to his feet and tried to dump me—which was a mistake on his part. I had been one of the strongest niggas on the football team. Instead of him picking me up, I picked him up and slammed him on the cement, knocking him out cold.

"Anybody else want their chance? Anybody!"

No one responded, so went and got in the car. I texted Donovan and told him I needed every piece of information he had on Diablo, and that I needed it now.

"Ross, you done moved up in life," Angie said.

We were at Angie's, and she was cooking some shrimp fried rice, shrimp egg rolls and sesame seed chicken.

"I'm doing okay," he grinned, showing us a mouthful of diamonds.

Ross was being modest. With JBM hitting all the D-boys in and round the city, Ross had took over a majority of the city. He no longer played the traps. All he did now was, meet Lauren and Karla, get the work and give it to Sha Loc. Sha Loc's crazy ass handled the distribution of the work, but even he didn't play the traps. He had slowed down too. He had recently gotten married to his girl Shereeya, and she had my nigga gone. Ross and Diqueena had hooked up some kind of way. I had sat him down, letting him know Diqueena was my baby and that if he wasn't going to treat her right, then to leave her alone. Ross had just bought a five-bedroom mansion, and was living the high life all the way around the board.

"The food is almost done." Angie sat down in my lap.

"Angie, you getting fat!" Murph teased.

"Shut up, Murph!" She threw one of the couch pillows at him.

"You are gaining weight, girl." I pinched her thick thighs through the Gucci leggings she had on.

"That's what happens when you're pregnant," she said, and the room got so quiet you could hear a mouse piss on a cotton ball.

"Congratulations!" Ross said to Angie, but he was looking at me.

"So what are y'all having?" Murph grinned.

"Who said it was his?" Angie asked.

I looked askance at Angie. She smiled.

"Murph, you know this Face baby," she took my hand and placed it on her stomach.

My mind was trying to process the news. Ross and Murph knew like I knew that Rai'chell was going to blow a head gasket.

"Let me go make y'all plates," she got up and walked in the kitchen.

"Bro, Rai'chell is going to kill you," Murph said.

"I know." I laid down on the couch, putting my forearm over my eyes.

This was going to create a new set of problems that I didn't need or want. The life of a street nigga!

Chapter Twenty-Seven

"Nigga, why you don't be coming to see me like that?" Laci asked.

I was sitting on her bed, looking over the information I had gotten from Donovan on Diablo. Diablo was twenty-nine, and was next up to run the Sinaloa Cartel with El Chapo locked up. The papers said Diablo controlled the top portion of Bragg Boulevard and all of Spring Lake, a city outside of Fayetteville. I needed to find a way to fuck up his cash flow but then again, that most likely wouldn't affect him. To go against him and come out on top was going to require a lot of finesse and luck. I couldn't simply overwhelm Diablo because he had more manpower than me. And he could replace his soldiers a hundred times faster than I could. My sacrifices were going to have to be well calculated. I was going to have to play the best game of chess I'd ever played.

"Laci, I got so many problems in my life right now it don't make no sense. I be coming over here to relax and clear my head. I know you're not going to aggravate and nag me but maybe I was wrong." I looked up from the papers.

"No, you're not wrong. I just be wanting to chill with you." She got down on the floor between my legs. "What kind of problems do you got, maybe I can help."

"I seriously doubt it, Laci." I took the blunt she had in her mouth, and filled my lungs.

"Nigga, don't doubt me! I helped you get that one dude's address and I got Kameesha's address and gave it to Murph. I've been helping you out for the longest without you even knowing it, so what kind of problems do you got?" she asked softly.

"I got beef with a high ranking cartel member, and as if that ain't enough, I got a baby on the way by another chick, so that's gonna create another major issue." I passed her the blunt and laid back.

Laci took the blunt, got up and straddled my lap.

"Rai'chell gon' trip, ain't she?"

"If only you know," I looked up at her.

"If you was my nigga, you wouldn't have to worry about me tripping over no petty shit like that."

"Is that right?"

"Hell yes! I can almost guarantee you she won't go to the lengths that I have for you," Laci said assuredly.

"I don't know about that one, ma. Rai'chell did some shit that if *anybody* else would have did, I woulda killed them."

Laci lowered her eyes into slits and said, "She wouldn't kill for you."

I didn't have my gun on me; it was in the living room, and I was thinking that leaving it there wasn't such a good idea.

The way Laci said her last statement made me uneasy.

"Would you kill for me?"

"I already have," she said, causing me to sit up but she pushed me back onto my back. "I'd never hurt you, Nymel," she said, as if reading my mind.

"What you mean you already have?"

Laci got up and went to her closet. She pulled a nurse uniform out and tossed it on the bed.

"I'm the one who killed Kameesha. I emptied an insulin-filled syringe in her IV."

Wow! The whole time I was under the assumption that Angie was the culprit, but it had been Laci.

"Bring yo ass here!"

I bent Laci over the bed, lifted the nightgown she had on, and fucked her to sleep.

"Bro, I got a lick for us!" Wolf said excitedly, walking into my office.

Me, Ross and Murph were in my office at *Pleasure's*, getting ready to meet Lauren and Karla. I couldn't wait to see Murph's face when they came in.

"Who?" Murph asked.

"Chief," he said, catching my attention.

Chief had been on my hit list forever! He supplied the entire Robeson County which consisted of about twenty cities. I knew for a fact he was sitting on at least ten million.

"How you stumble up on that?" I was curious.

"He's Pocahontas' brother."

They were both Native Americans, so I could see it. It made sense. She told me her brother spoiled her, but I would have never guessed it to be Chief though.

"Do you have the inside scoop?" asked Murph.

"I'm working on it."

I wasn't going to take part in the lick. I was just going to let JBM do it. I would still reap the benefits. Wolf walked out as Lauren and Karla walked in.

"What the fuck!" Murph stood up.

"Chill, bro," I laughed.

"Hey, y'all!" Lauren said, walked behind the desk where I was, and sat on the edge of the desk. "You have a serious problem on your hands."

"What are you talking about?" I asked.

"Diablo."

"How the fuck you know about that?" I narrowed my eyes.

"Come on. Let's talk." She grabbed my hand.

I let her lead me out of the office. I couldn't help but stare at Lauren's amazon ass, which turned more heads than the naked strippers. At 5'11 she was almost as tall as me, with this evenly proportioned body. Her mocha complexion was blemish-free, and her full titties sat up high and perky in her white sweater. She had real chinky eyes with long eyelashes, and silky black hair that hung to the middle of her back. But her ass held my attention because it was moving like a cup of jello. Karla was built the same way.

"Can we go up there?" she asked of one of the empty VIP sections, and I nodded.

We sat down on one of the couches, and she turned to face me.

"Face, had you treated me any differently that night at Karma's, I wouldn't even be doing this. But you're the reason we're on. We took the money from Karma's safe and took it to the plug. You know Karma had me meeting the plug and bringing the work back down here, so me and the plug were already familiar with each other. Listen, the plug—whose name is Chino—is also a part of the Sinaloa Cartel. Chino wants Diablo out of the way so he can be the next head of the cartel.

"Let me guess. He's going to help me kill him."

"Yes but it benefits all of us. It would make Ross the main supplier of heroin in the city, you wouldn't have any more beef, and Chino would be next in line for his cartel."

"What do you get though?"

"Money! The more money Ross makes, the more money I make."

I nodded. To not accept the help would be crazy. Like the old saying went, the enemy of my enemy is a friend to me.

Chapter Twenty-Eight

With Lauren's revelation about her plug willing to help me get rid of Diablo, I was able to breathe easier. I knew Diablo would be dealt with in the near future, so that left me to deal with Angie and the news about her being pregnant.

"You know I thought you were the one that had killed Kameesha."

"I was going to, but I was too late. When I went in that night, they said someone had given her the wrong medicine. Then it came out that she had received a lethal dose of insulin. With no immediate family to press the issue, the hospital was able to sweep it under the rug."

"Are you really pregnant, Angie?" I asked, watching her brush her long hair at the dresser.

"I'm going to act like you didn't ask me that. You know I wouldn't have allowed myself to go like this."

She had a point, I thought to myself, looking at the bulge she was sporting in her blue romper.

"Nah, baby, I just thought you might have been playing, that's all."

"I know Rai'chell is going to trip and you know I'm not trying to mess up your relationship, so you can tell her the baby isn't yours. But that doesn't mean you can neglect your duties as a father."

I got up and walked over to her. I grabbed her by the neck and said, "Don't try to play me like that. I'm a man, so I can accept the consequences of my actions. I'll never deny a child that's mine."

"I love you, Nymel," her eyes got watery.

"Love you more."

I sat back on the bed and grabbed my phone. I was getting all kinds of texts from TNT. I got a video text showing Golden

Gate trailer park up in flames! All I could do was smile. They didn't play; if someone did harm to one of their people, retaliation was swift and deadly. I looked up as a naked Angie walked between my legs and pushed me back onto the bed. Her deep caramel-colored body turned me on to no end. She placed her pretty pink lips on mine, then climbed up my body until I was face to face with her pretty pussy. I kissed her pussy lips, and they opened up. I ran my tongue from the bottom to the top, stopping to suck her enlarged clit into my mouth.

"Nymeeel" Angie moaned.

I began circling her clit with my tongue, causing Angie to rock her hips.

"I'm about to cum, Nymel," she whispered.

I drew my name in cursive on her clit, earning a face full of Angie's love juices. I got up from under her, and crawled between her legs. I pushed into her love tunnel, and almost lost it. I had forgot how wet pregnant pussy was. I was mid-stroke when my phone rang with Tasha's ringtone. I ignored it; Angie's pussy had me in the headlock.

"You feel so good, Nymel!' Angie pulled her hair.

Tasha called me right back.

"Ughh!" I paused, and reached over to grab my phone. "What?"

"Your homeboy is going to be released in the next hour," Tasha informed me.

"A'ight." I hung up.

Angie was looking up at me with a *nigga-you-can't-be-serious* look.

"That was my lawyer, baby." I cradled her, and rolled over so that she was on top.

"I love you, boy." Angie leaned down, putting her head in the crook of my neck.

I grabbed her ass with both hands, spread her cheeks apart, and started pushing up into her at a rapid pace. The squishing sounds her box was making every time I lifted my hips let me know I was doing my thing.

"*Babbyyy!*" She moaned into my neck.

Angie tried to run, but I gripped her ass tighter, holding her in place.

"Fuck!" I coated Angie's walls with more babies.

We laid there, reveling in the aftermath of our quickie.

"What did your lawyer want?" she asked lazily.

"She was letting me know that my man is about to get out of jail, so I gotta go pick him up. Let me go."

Angie groaned but rolled off of me.

"You coming back?" She watched as I put my clothes on.

"Of course. I need some more of that coochie. That was only an appetizer."

"Noooo!" Angie put her hand between her legs, rolling around on the bed, being goofy.

"You silly," I kissed her on the forehead and walked out.

With Ox being released, he could take TNT back over and lift another weight off my shoulders, leaving me to focus on more important matters.

I pulled my Porsche into the jail, and parked. It was a bright, sunny day, but it was cold as hell! November wasn't playing any games, and the weatherman said it was going to snow. As I waited for Ox to walk out, I saw Corrigan come walking out the county. Corrigan got in his truck and pulled over to me.

"What up?" I rolled my window down.

"Here," he handed me five more folders.

"A'ight." I tossed them on the seat, and he rode off. I was getting five to eight folders a week. And now they were involving D-boys outside of Fayetteville. Two days ago, Maino had hit a weed man for thirty pounds of sour diesel.

I cut on Kodak Black's "Last Day In" when I saw Ox walk out the county. My nigga hadn't gained one pound. He was still skinny as hell. I blew the horn, getting his attention. He smiled and ran over, getting in the car.

"Damn, I ain't think I was ever gonna walk out them doors again."

"Now that you're a free man, what's the plan?"

"Get the bag and terrorize shit! Ain't shit changed, my nigga, but the year."

I laughed and shook my head. "I ain't mad at you, but make sure you use your head now. Ain't shit cool about being locked up and having to depend on somebody else."

"That's a fact, but I also know that jail and prison is a part of the lifestyle we live. For me to think otherwise would be me living in denial."

I couldn't disagree with him because what he said was true. Jail or prison came with the street life, the only thing that differed was the amount of time you did. Some got blessed, and only got a few years to do. Some never were going to come home again.

"What are these folders?" Ox flipped through them.

"Stings. Go ahead and pick you one. That's gon' put you all the way on your feet," I urged.

"Got one! Hell yea, he up too, I been hearing about this nigga."

"Let me see," I smiled. "Oh shit!" My face darkened, seeing the face inside the folder.

"What up, bro?"

"That's my day one—Ross."

To Be Continued…
Confessions of a Jackboy 3
Coming Soon

Lock Down Publications and Ca$h Presents assisted
publishing packages.

BASIC PACKAGE $499
Editing
Cover Design
Formatting

UPGRADED PACKAGE $800
Typing
Editing
Cover Design
Formatting

ADVANCE PACKAGE $1,200
Typing
Editing
Cover Design
Formatting
Copyright registration
Proofreading
Upload book to Amazon

LDP SUPREME PACKAGE $1,500
Typing
Editing
Cover Design
Formatting
Copyright registration
Proofreading

Set up Amazon account
Upload book to Amazon
Advertise on LDP Amazon and Facebook page

***Other services available upon request. Additional
charges may apply
Lock Down Publications
P.O. Box 944
Stockbridge, GA 30281-9998
Phone # 470 303-9761

Submission Guideline

Submit the first three chapters of your completed manuscript to ldpsubmissions@gmail.com, subject line: Your book's title. The manuscript must be in a .doc file and sent as an attachment. Document should be in Times New Roman, double spaced and in size 12 font. Also, provide your synopsis and full contact information. If sending multiple submissions, they must each be in a separate email.

Have a story but no way to send it electronically? You can still submit to LDP/Ca$h Presents. Send in the first three chapters, written or typed, of your completed manuscript to:

LDP: Submissions Dept
Po Box 944
Stockbridge, Ga 30281

DO NOT send original manuscript. Must be a duplicate.

Provide your synopsis and a cover letter containing your full contact information.

Thanks for considering LDP and Ca$h Presents.

<u>NEW RELEASES</u>

LOYAL TO THE SOIL by JIBRIL WILLIAMS
A GANGSTA'S PAIN by J-BLUNT
MONEY IN THE GRAVE 2 by MARTELL
"TROUBLESOME" BOLDEN
THE BRICK MAN 2 by KING RIO
A DOPEBOY'S DREAM 3 by ROMELL TUKES
CONFESSIONS OF A JACKBOY II by NICHO-
LAS LOCK

Coming Soon from Lock Down Publications/Ca$h Presents

BLOOD OF A BOSS **VI**

SHADOWS OF THE GAME II

TRAP BASTARD II

By **Askari**

LOYAL TO THE GAME **IV**

By **T.J. & Jelissa**

IF TRUE SAVAGE **VIII**

MIDNIGHT CARTEL IV

DOPE BOY MAGIC IV

CITY OF KINGZ III

NIGHTMARE ON SILENT AVE II

By **Chris Green**

BLAST FOR ME **III**

A SAVAGE DOPEBOY III

CUTTHROAT MAFIA III

DUFFLE BAG CARTEL VII

HEARTLESS GOON VI

By **Ghost**

A HUSTLER'S DECEIT III

KILL ZONE II

BAE BELONGS TO ME III

By **Aryanna**

KING OF THE TRAP III

By **T.J. Edwards**

GORILLAZ IN THE BAY V

3X KRAZY III

STRAIGHT BEAST MODE II

De'Kari

KINGPIN KILLAZ IV

STREET KINGS III

PAID IN BLOOD III

CARTEL KILLAZ IV

DOPE GODS III

Hood Rich

SINS OF A HUSTLA II

ASAD

RICH $AVAGE II

MONEY IN THE GRAVE II

By Martell Troublesome Bolden

YAYO V

Bred In The Game 2

S. Allen

CREAM III

By Yolanda Moore

SON OF A DOPE FIEND III

HEAVEN GOT A GHETTO II

By Renta

LOYALTY AIN'T PROMISED III

By Keith Williams

I'M NOTHING WITHOUT HIS LOVE II

SINS OF A THUG II

TO THE THUG I LOVED BEFORE II

By Monet Dragun

Nicholas Lock

QUIET MONEY IV

EXTENDED CLIP III

THUG LIFE IV

By **Trai'Quan**

THE STREETS MADE ME IV

By **Larry D. Wright**

IF YOU CROSS ME ONCE II

By **Anthony Fields**

THE STREETS WILL NEVER CLOSE II

By **K'ajji**

HARD AND RUTHLESS III

THE BILLIONAIRE BENTLEYS II

Von Diesel

KILLA KOUNTY II

By **Khufu**

MONEY GAME III

By **Smoove Dolla**

A GANGSTA'S KARMA II

By **FLAME**

JACK BOYZ VERSUS DOPE BOYZ

By **Romell Tukes**

MURDA WAS THE CASE II

Elijah R. Freeman

THE STREETS NEVER LET GO II

By **Robert Baptiste**

AN UNFORESEEN LOVE III

By **Meesha**

KING OF THE TRENCHES II
by **GHOST & TRANAY ADAMS**

MONEY MAFIA II

LOYAL TO THE SOIL II

By **Jibril Williams**

QUEEN OF THE ZOO II

By **Black Migo**

THE BRICK MAN III

By **King Rio**

VICIOUS LOYALTY II

By **Kingpen**

A GANGSTA'S PAIN II

By **J-Blunt**

CONFESSIONS OF A JACKBOY III

By **Nicholas Lock**

<u>Available Now</u>

RESTRAINING ORDER **I & II**

By **CA$H & Coffee**

LOVE KNOWS NO BOUNDARIES **I II & III**

Nicholas Lock

By **Coffee**
RAISED AS A GOON I, II, III & IV
BRED BY THE SLUMS I, II, III
BLAST FOR ME I & II
ROTTEN TO THE CORE I II III
A BRONX TALE I, II, III
DUFFLE BAG CARTEL I II III IV V VI
HEARTLESS GOON I II III IV V
A SAVAGE DOPEBOY I II
DRUG LORDS I II III
CUTTHROAT MAFIA I II
KING OF THE TRENCHES
By **Ghost**
LAY IT DOWN **I & II**
LAST OF A DYING BREED I II
BLOOD STAINS OF A SHOTTA I & II III
By **Jamaica**
LOYAL TO THE GAME I II III
LIFE OF SIN I, II III
By **TJ & Jelissa**
BLOODY COMMAS I & II
SKI MASK CARTEL I II & III
KING OF NEW YORK I II,III IV V
RISE TO POWER I II III
COKE KINGS I II III IV V
BORN HEARTLESS I II III IV
KING OF THE TRAP I II

By **T.J. Edwards**
IF LOVING HIM IS WRONG…I & II
LOVE ME EVEN WHEN IT HURTS I II III
By **Jelissa**
WHEN THE STREETS CLAP BACK I & II III
THE HEART OF A SAVAGE I II III
MONEY MAFIA
LOYAL TO THE SOIL
By **Jibril Williams**
A DISTINGUISHED THUG STOLE MY HEART I II & III
LOVE SHOULDN'T HURT I II III IV
RENEGADE BOYS I II III IV
PAID IN KARMA I II III
SAVAGE STORMS I II
AN UNFORESEEN LOVE I II
By **Meesha**
A GANGSTER'S CODE I &, II III
A GANGSTER'S SYN I II III
THE SAVAGE LIFE I II III
CHAINED TO THE STREETS I II III
BLOOD ON THE MONEY I II III
A GANGSTA'S PAIN
By **J-Blunt**
PUSH IT TO THE LIMIT
By **Bre' Hayes**
BLOOD OF A BOSS **I, II, III, IV, V**
SHADOWS OF THE GAME

Nicholas Lock

TRAP BASTARD

By **Askari**

THE STREETS BLEED MURDER **I, II & III**

THE HEART OF A GANGSTA I II& III

By **Jerry Jackson**

CUM FOR ME I II III IV V VI VII

An **LDP Erotica Collaboration**

BRIDE OF A HUSTLA **I II & II**

THE FETTI GIRLS **I, II& III**

CORRUPTED BY A GANGSTA I, II III, IV

BLINDED BY HIS LOVE

THE PRICE YOU PAY FOR LOVE I, II ,III

DOPE GIRL MAGIC I II III

By **Destiny Skai**

WHEN A GOOD GIRL GOES BAD

By **Adrienne**

THE COST OF LOYALTY I II III

By Kweli

A GANGSTER'S REVENGE **I II III & IV**

THE BOSS MAN'S DAUGHTERS I II III IV V

A SAVAGE LOVE **I & II**

BAE BELONGS TO ME I II

A HUSTLER'S DECEIT I, II, III

WHAT BAD BITCHES DO I, II, III

SOUL OF A MONSTER I II III

KILL ZONE

A DOPE BOY'S QUEEN I II III

By **Aryanna**
A KINGPIN'S AMBITON
A KINGPIN'S AMBITION **II**
I MURDER FOR THE DOUGH
By **Ambitious**
TRUE SAVAGE I II III IV V VI VII
DOPE BOY MAGIC I, II, III
MIDNIGHT CARTEL I II III
CITY OF KINGZ I II
NIGHTMARE ON SILENT AVE
By **Chris Green**
A DOPEBOY'S PRAYER
By **Eddie "Wolf" Lee**
THE KING CARTEL **I, II & III**
By **Frank Gresham**
THESE NIGGAS AIN'T LOYAL **I, II & III**
By **Nikki Tee**
GANGSTA SHYT **I II &III**
By **CATO**
THE ULTIMATE BETRAYAL
By **Phoenix**
BOSS'N UP **I , II & III**
By **Royal Nicole**
I LOVE YOU TO DEATH
By **Destiny J**
I RIDE FOR MY HITTA
I STILL RIDE FOR MY HITTA

By **Misty Holt**

LOVE & CHASIN' PAPER

By **Qay Crockett**

TO DIE IN VAIN

SINS OF A HUSTLA

By **ASAD**

BROOKLYN HUSTLAZ

By **Boogsy Morina**

BROOKLYN ON LOCK I & II

By **Sonovia**

GANGSTA CITY

By **Teddy Duke**

A DRUG KING AND HIS DIAMOND I & II III

A DOPEMAN'S RICHES

HER MAN, MINE'S TOO I, II

CASH MONEY HO'S

THE WIFEY I USED TO BE I II

By **Nicole Goosby**

TRAPHOUSE KING **I II & III**

KINGPIN KILLAZ I II III

STREET KINGS I II

PAID IN BLOOD **I II**

CARTEL KILLAZ I II III

DOPE GODS I II

By **Hood Rich**

LIPSTICK KILLAH **I, II, III**

CRIME OF PASSION I II & III

FRIEND OR FOE I II III

By **Mimi**

STEADY MOBBN' **I, II, III**

THE STREETS STAINED MY SOUL I II

By **Marcellus Allen**

WHO SHOT YA **I, II, III**

SON OF A DOPE FIEND I II

HEAVEN GOT A GHETTO

Renta

GORILLAZ IN THE BAY **I II III IV**

TEARS OF A GANGSTA I II

3X KRAZY I II

STRAIGHT BEAST MODE

DE'KARI

TRIGGADALE I II III

MURDAROBER WAS THE CASE

Elijah R. Freeman

GOD BLESS THE TRAPPERS I, II, III

THESE SCANDALOUS STREETS I, II, III

FEAR MY GANGSTA I, II, III IV, V

THESE STREETS DON'T LOVE NOBODY I, II

BURY ME A G I, II, III, IV, V

A GANGSTA'S EMPIRE I, II, III, IV

THE DOPEMAN'S BODYGAURD I II

THE REALEST KILLAZ I II III

THE LAST OF THE OGS I II III

Tranay Adams

THE STREETS ARE CALLING

Duquie Wilson

MARRIED TO A BOSS I II III

By Destiny Skai & Chris Green

KINGZ OF THE GAME I II III IV V VI

Playa Ray

SLAUGHTER GANG I II III

RUTHLESS HEART I II III

By Willie Slaughter

FUK SHYT

By Blakk Diamond

DON'T F#CK WITH MY HEART I II

By Linnea

ADDICTED TO THE DRAMA I II III

IN THE ARM OF HIS BOSS II

By Jamila

YAYO I II III IV

A SHOOTER'S AMBITION I II

BRED IN THE GAME

By S. Allen

TRAP GOD I II III

RICH $AVAGE

MONEY IN THE GRAVE I II

By Martell Troublesome Bolden

FOREVER GANGSTA

GLOCKS ON SATIN SHEETS I II

By Adrian Dulan

TOE TAGZ I II III

LEVELS TO THIS SHYT I II

By Ah'Million

KINGPIN DREAMS I II III

By Paper Boi Rari

CONFESSIONS OF A GANGSTA I II III IV

CONFESSIONS OF A JACKBOY I II

By Nicholas Lock

I'M NOTHING WITHOUT HIS LOVE

SINS OF A THUG

TO THE THUG I LOVED BEFORE

By Monet Dragun

CAUGHT UP IN THE LIFE I II III

THE STREETS NEVER LET GO

By Robert Baptiste

NEW TO THE GAME I II III

MONEY, MURDER & MEMORIES I II III

By **Malik D. Rice**

LIFE OF A SAVAGE I II III

A GANGSTA'S QUR'AN I II III

MURDA SEASON I II III

GANGLAND CARTEL I II III

CHI'RAQ GANGSTAS I II III

KILLERS ON ELM STREET I II III

JACK BOYZ N DA BRONX I II III

A DOPEBOY'S DREAM I II III

By Romell Tukes

LOYALTY AIN'T PROMISED I II

By Keith Williams

QUIET MONEY I II III

THUG LIFE I II III

EXTENDED CLIP I II

By **Trai'Quan**

THE STREETS MADE ME I II III

By **Larry D. Wright**

THE ULTIMATE SACRIFICE I, II, III, IV, V, VI

KHADIFI

IF YOU CROSS ME ONCE

ANGEL I II

IN THE BLINK OF AN EYE

By **Anthony Fields**

THE LIFE OF A HOOD STAR

By Ca$h & Rashia Wilson

THE STREETS WILL NEVER CLOSE

By K'ajji

CREAM I II

By Yolanda Moore

NIGHTMARES OF A HUSTLA I II III

By King Dream

CONCRETE KILLA I II

VICIOUS LOYALTY

By Kingpen

HARD AND RUTHLESS I II

MOB TOWN 251

THE BILLIONAIRE BENTLEYS

By Von Diesel

GHOST MOB

Stilloan Robinson

MOB TIES I II III IV

By SayNoMore

BODYMORE MURDERLAND I II III

By Delmont Player

FOR THE LOVE OF A BOSS

By C. D. Blue

MOBBED UP I II III IV

THE BRICK MAN I II

By King Rio

KILLA KOUNTY

By Khufu

MONEY GAME I II

By Smoove Dolla

A GANGSTA'S KARMA

By FLAME

KING OF THE TRENCHES II

by **GHOST & TRANAY ADAMS**

QUEEN OF THE ZOO

By **Black Migo**

BOOKS BY LDP'S CEO, CA$H

TRUST IN NO MAN

TRUST IN NO MAN 2

TRUST IN NO MAN 3

BONDED BY BLOOD

SHORTY GOT A THUG

THUGS CRY

THUGS CRY 2

THUGS CRY 3

TRUST NO BITCH

TRUST NO BITCH 2

TRUST NO BITCH 3

TIL MY CASKET DROPS

RESTRAINING ORDER

RESTRAINING ORDER 2

IN LOVE WITH A CONVICT

LIFE OF A HOOD STAR

Confessions of a Jackboy 2